Deadly Revenge

ANGUS BRODIE AND MIKAELA FORSYTHE MURDER MYSTERY
BOOK FIFTEEN

CARLA SIMPSON

OLIVERHEBERBOOKS

Prologue

IT WAS COLD, the sort of cold that settled in the bones this time of year in spite of the thick wool of Constable Joseph Martin's thick wool overcoat.

Not that he wasn't used to it after more than twenty years on the street. Still, he thought, he must be getting old as he rolled his shoulders against the stiffness that had set in.

It was late, very near midnight he guessed, most of the lights about the 'Circus' dimmed as taverns had closed, shops completely darkened, the last lights of the theater district winking out in the distance through the misty fog.

The usually well-lit sign for Mellins Food had gone out hours ago and was barely visible across from the roundabout with the recently added statue in the center.

A Greek God it was said, with bow and arrow, to commemorate the Earl of Shaftsbury for his charity work.

Constable Martin figured it wouldn't take long for someone to remove the arrow, young louts in a prank no doubt. And then the arrow would show up at some other location in some offensive manner.

"I'll see you the next street over," Constable Tabor, his partner said, in what had become their nightly routine.

They would each make one last circle around in opposite directions, Regent Street, then a last stretch down Shaftsbury on his usual patrol of the night, as Tabor came back around where they would meet and end their shift.

It was far easier that way to cover the 'Circus' one last time during the late shift. And truth be told, there was rarely any activity on the street this late, other than a shopkeeper who had stayed late closing for the night.

But apparently not tonight, as Constable Martin glanced down the street, with faint pools of light from the streetlamps that were swallowed by the grey shroud of mist that had rolled in from the river.

He checked the pocket watch he carried in the thin light of a nearby streetlamp. It was almost midnight. With one last turn, he would be home by one o'clock and warm in bed after signing out at the station house. He pocketed his watch.

"Cor! But it's bloody cold enough to freeze the balls off a brass monkey," his partner exclaimed.

"Step lively, then," Joseph Martin said in parting as each set off. "And we'll be done for the night.

Only a handful of years more, and then he would have his pension, thanks to the new system that had been created for those with long-term service.

His Maddy had been frugal over the years and had also worked in a bakery shop. There was a good amount saved. They might open a shop of their own. At night he could close the door against the cold instead of walking the streets.

Perhaps dry goods, he thought, as he started down Regent Street. Or a bake shop for tarts and cakes. His Maddy was talented that way.

Customers came from all parts of London for her fruit-filled tarts and cakes. And he had no complaint for the early hours required in a bake shop after walking patrol late at night.

He could almost feel the warmth of the bakery ovens as he reached the end of the block then turned at the corner. That had a far greater appeal than dry goods for certain.

They had talked about it before, perhaps even taking over the bake shop when he was able to finally step away from the MET. The man she worked for was getting on in years; he might be open to the idea.

Only a little farther now until he met Constable Tabor back at the roundabout, then on to the Vine Street station, a bit of a walk farther on the last part of their patrol.

A sound had him turning about, then he shook his head at the creature that darted out from the narrow alleyway and immediately dove into a narrow crack in the stone steps of a darkened shop.

"A bit cold even for the likes of you," he commented as he gathered the collar of his coat closer and continued on. Not even the rats wanted to be out on this night.

"Constable Martin."

It was faint at first, followed by the sound of footsteps. Then closer.

"Joseph Martin..."

"Aye?"

He turned as a shadow stepped out from the coved entrance of a shop and slowly came toward him.

"Who might you be, sir?"

That rasping voice obviously belonged to a man, although it was low, barely more than a whisper.

There was no response, only those steps and the shadow that approached, then stopped less than two feet away.

The man wore a long coat, a hat with the brim pulled low, and a neck scarf. Not the usual sort found in the west end, although he might have been a worker finding his way home late.

"Do you remember me?" That voice reached through the cold night air.

Remember? What the devil, Constable Martin thought. The man must have had too much of the drink.

"It's no night to be out and about," he replied. "Best that you get on home."

"There is no home," came the response. "No one there. They're all gone."

All gone? No one there?

"If you've a need of a cab...?" he started to say, then saw the dull gleam of the knife.

He stepped back too late. The knife thrust through the thick wool of his coat, then deeper, followed by sharp pain as he struck out to push the man away. Warmth spread beneath his coat where there had been only the cold, and the air clogged in his throat.

His fist closed over the front of the man's coat as he fought to bring up his truncheon. In the struggle the man's scarf was lost.

"Do you remember now?" the man hissed at him as he bent over him.

Constable Martin saw the marled flesh at the man's neck, the icy glare in that narrowed gaze. A memory returned and recognition came with it.

"You!"

There was a slow, cold smile as his killer stepped away from him, and Constable Martin slumped to the sidewalk and watched with dying eyes as the man bent, retrieved the scarf, then slowly walked away.

One

BRODIE AND FORSYTHE PRIVATE
INQUIRIES, #204 THE STRAND, LONDON

ANGUS BRODIE SAT across from Inspector Dooley, an elbow propped on the arm of the desk chair as he frowned at the news his friend brought.

"I thought you should know straight away."

The accent from the man's birth in Ireland was there. It wrapped around the words, with the gravity of the matter. The same as the first day they had worked together when Brodie was just a new recruit fresh from training. And then later as inspector with the Metropolitan.

'Blue Devils' the recruits were called then and included a new identity from the one he'd carried from Edinburgh. Along with skills acquired on the streets that offered experience that couldna' be found otherwise, and the cold determination burnin' in his belly to make something of himself before the streets decided otherwise.

Then, he'd walked the streets with Joseph Martin, older by ten years and with a good amount of experience, who gradually chipped away at the anger and resentment that Brodie had wrapped around himself like a protective shield.

7

Much like an older brother, Martin taught and protected him, at times from himself, and then stood with pride and watched years later when Brodie became inspector of police.

"I belong on the streets," Joe had told him then. *"I wouldn't know what to do with myself in a suit of regular clothes, investigating crimes, questioning witnesses. But you have the head for it.*

"You see things in people. You know a lie when you hear it, and you have friends in places where most wouldn't go.

"I'm proud of you, Brodie, although I wouldn't have bet good money that you would survive those first months you walked with me, charging into places and situations as if the devil was on your tail."

"When did it happen?" Brodie asked now, as he pushed that memory back.

"His shift last night," Mr. Dooley replied.

Another good man, who'd understood when Brodie had to walk away from the person who threatened to take everything away that he'd achieved and start over again with private inquiries.

"Witnesses?"

Dooley shook his head. "None that time of the night. His partner, Constable Tabor, found him when he failed to meet at the end of their shift and he backtracked to Regent Street."

Brodie frowned. It was not the first time that a constable had been attacked and killed in the line of duty, yet it hadn't happened in some time as far as he knew. Still, a constable by himself? It was the reason two usually covered their area.

"There might be something to be learned on the street," he commented, his thoughts already going to those who worked the street in a different manner, the underground information system controlled by organized gangs that was well known among those who served the MET.

Still, late in the night, and at Piccadilly with most people well gone for the evenin'? Not a time of the night when targets for robbery were plentiful.

"Has there been a report from any of the shop owners and businesses in the area about a burglary?"

Mr. Dooley shook his head. "Nothing that has been reported."

"Wot of the attack?"

"A long-blade was used, a single deep wound according to the police surgeon. It was over very quick. There didn't seem to be any sign of a struggle beforehand."

Brodie's dark gaze narrowed. No struggle. That was not like the man he knew.

He thought of possible motive. "Was anything taken?"

"He still had his watch on him along with a few coins."

No struggle and not for robbery.

"That could be useful."

He thought then of Joe's wife and the warm suppers she had insisted he share with them instead of returning each night to a cold flat.

"What of his wife?"

"She knows, but I thought considerin'..." his voice trailed off. There was no need to explain.

Brodie nodded. "I will call on her. Wot of the service?"

There would be one as soon as the police surgeon released the body.

Joseph Martin had served nearly twenty-five years with the Metropolitan Police, a tenure that had included several commendations, as well as being highly respected by all those who worked with him. There would undoubtedly be an honor guard out of respect, though it was not a common practice.

"That will be determined later. I will let you know when we have word on that."

"Mr. Conner should be made aware as well," Brodie added. "I will speak with him, although he may already know of it from some of other lads."

"Aye, they served some time together."

"Who is on the case?" Brodie inquired.

There was a brotherhood among those who served the MET, particularly those who walked the streets. When something like this happened, they would want answers, and the person caught who was responsible.

"It's not been assigned yet." Dooley's gaze sharpened. "I came to tell you as soon as word came down this morning because of the time you spent with him on the street.

"No doubt Abberline will see to the matter."

Abberline. Formally reprimanded with time away and now returned as Chief Inspector. He saw the look Dooley gave him.

"It's best to let others handle this for reasons you know well enough."

Brodie made no response. There were good people with the MET, Mr. Dooley was one of them. But as he knew all too well, they were short of staff, and their hands were often tied by those they answered to.

A sound came from the landing outside the office. Dooley stood to leave.

"As I said, it's best to let others handle this. I'll send word when the day for the service is announced," he added as the door opened and Mikaela Forsythe entered the office.

Mr. Dooley tipped the brim of his hat in greeting. Then, with a look at Brodie, left.

MIKAELA

"Mr. Dooley seemed most serious. Is there some difficulty?" I commented as he left with a serious expression and a brief nod. Very much out of character for the man.

"A matter he wanted me to know about," Brodie replied. "A man I worked with when I was with the MET was attacked and killed last night."

To anyone else, the way he said it would have seemed unemotional, matter-of-fact, a bit of news, nothing more. It was much like listening to someone giving a report.

Yet, I sensed something else, in that way I had learned. There was most definitely something more there.

Brodie was not one to allow his emotions to show. A habit learned through early loss on the streets of Edinburgh, before he came to London, I could only assume.

However, in the time we had worked together, I had learned to sense things in a mannerism, the way a mask—his police inspector demeanor from his years with the MET—slipped into place. It was there now.

I watched as he neatly gathered several papers together, then tucked them into a folder, his mouth a straight line.

He rose from behind the desk, then went to the file cabinet and put the folder away. And it was there, that hint of his conversation with Mr. Dooley in the less-than-subtle slam of the cabinet drawer.

"You knew the man well?" I inquired.

"It's difficult not to know someone when ye walk the streets with 'em for more than four years," he bit off.

I sensed the undercurrent of pain and saw the anger in the dark brows that drew together over his dark gaze.

There had been few in his life whom he'd respected or

trusted. His friend Munro was one who came from Edinburgh with him all those years before. And oddly enough it also included my great-aunt, Lady Antonia Montgomery. That was a most interesting situation. And then there was myself.

We had learned to trust one another through the various cases we had pursued. And then there was the respect.

In spite of my resolve to remain an unmarried woman, there had been an undeniable attraction. We might have carried on as some did, but he would not have it and had proposed marriage, taking me by surprise.

He was undeniably a handsome man, tall, with dark hair and beard, dark eyes, and the look of someone who could be dangerous if he chose. And there was that other thing that had come highly recommended, from my great-aunt of all persons.

"Constable Martin?" I asked, guessing the victim must be the man he had spoken of often. Someone who, as Brodie explained, had saved him from himself, curbing his reckless-ness, a habit of rushing into a situation that he had learned on the streets.

"Last night, near the Circus."

I was aware how much he respected Constable Martin, as well as trusted him, and sensed the deep loss.

"There will be a service," he added. "Mr. Dooley will let me know when that will be."

"He was married," I knew that as well from conversations about those early days with the MET.

He looked at me for the first time, and I saw the pain there.

From what he had told me, Constable Martin and his wife never had children. I didn't know about other family, but I sensed that he might have been very close with both of them.

"I will call on his wife when it's appropriate."

I touched his shoulder and could feel the tension beneath the fabric of his shirt.

"I should think that she might want to hear from you now."

The mask slipped. I saw his answer in the way the anger left that dark gaze.

"I could send round a message."

"Or you might simply call on her."

His mouth worked with what might have been an excuse to put it off until later, then thinned as if it was a physical pain.

I did wonder how many times he had called on other widows in his time with the Metropolitan, forced to maintain a certain demeanor. But now for a friend? I laid my hand at his arm.

We had both experienced painful losses. It was never easy, but this seemed to be especially difficult.

"Aye," he eventually replied.

"I will go with you."

I saw his answer in that dark gaze as he laid his hand over mine.

He had Mr. Cavendish wave down a cab and we departed for Braxton Place near Covent Garden where Constable Martin and his wife lived.

The block of flats at Braxton Place was like many throughout London's working-class areas, with grey stone facades at three-story buildings, the landlord's flat on the ground floor, and a dozen or more flats on the floors above.

Yet contrary to many residential flats, the building at Number 8 Braxton Place was neat and well maintained, with concrete steps that led from the sidewalk.

Brodie assisted me down from the cab.

The Martins had lived there for several years, and he knew it well.

"Number 4B at the second floor," he said as we entered the foyer of the building.

The entrance was neat and well-kept, with letter boxes on the wall to the left of the entrance, each with a flat number on the outside.

He went to the door beside those letter boxes and knocked. A short man with grey hair answered the door. Brodie informed him that we were there to see Mrs. Martin. He nodded.

"Sad news this mornin', Mr. Brodie. The police were round first thing. Constable Martin was a good man. She's been up there since. Didn't go to work as usual. Understandable."

It was obvious the landlord remembered him.

"A man just doing his job and then killed for it. Do the police know who did it?" he asked.

"Not as yet, and I thank ye for yer time, sir," Brodie replied. He turned then and wrapped a hand around my arm.

We easily found flat 4B on the second floor and Brodie knocked.

It was several moments before Mrs. Martin appeared and I thought she might have decided that she didn't want to see anyone. Then the door slowly opened.

Maddy Martin was a small woman with a round face, sad blue eyes, and a smile that trembled at the sight of Brodie.

The tears came then as she opened the door further. She reached for the edge of her apron.

"Oh, Angus."

. . .

We sat in the small sitting room beside the kitchen. There, at a narrow side table was a sepia-toned photograph of Constable Martin in uniform when he received one of his commendations. There was a second photograph beside it of a half-dozen uniformed constables, standing shoulder to shoulder, that included Brodie.

We had met after he left the MET and established his inquiry business. I had never seen him in a uniform.

He was quite a bit younger then, handsome to be certain, and with an almost defiant look in those dark eyes.

He had changed, of course, through the years since. Where there had been defiance, there was at times now a certain coldness with faint lines at the corners of his eyes.

Perhaps from things experienced, I thought. Yet in a way that only emphasized the impression that here was a man who knew far more than he let on, and one that others might not want to cross.

"I knew that you had married," Maddy said, surprising me with a sad smile. "He spoke of it and said that it was a good thing, that a man needed someone in that way. A titled lady, and pretty too. I hear you assist in his inquiry cases."

"When he allows it," I explained.

"Oh, it's the Scot in him," she replied with a faint smile over at Brodie. "Stubborn."

"Oh, yes," I replied.

"Do ye have wot ye need here?" Brodie asked then.

"I don't need anything, except..." Maddy replied. Her voice caught.

I knew what she would have said, that she needed her husband.

"I will bring round food that ye'll need," Brodie said. "Wot of the rents?"

She shook her head. "We had money saved for after he retired. It will carry me a while, and everyone here has been more than kind and brought food, as you can see." She was quiet then.

"I've always known the work could be dangerous, but I want to know what happened. I want the person responsible found. Do you hear what I say, Angus Brodie?"

Steel wrapped in silk. I thought of that saying. I was hearing it now, sadness and determination.

"I know the men will do their best," she said. "But I know from him, there are places they cannot go and things that simply get swept under the rug. He spoke of it, and you know as well." She took a breath, calm, measured when she spoke again.

"I know your services must be very expensive. But you can make inquiries in those places. I will work the rest of my life to pay your fee if you will find the person who did this."

I knew what his answer would be before he spoke. He would take the case and make inquiries. And there would be no fee.

"I promise ye. I will find the one responsible."

Two

OUR RIDE back to the office was quiet except for sounds from the street.

I knew his thoughts were already filled with questions over Constable Martin's death, as well as the inquiries he would now make among those he knew.

Along with that was the sadness and grief over the loss of a man he had respected and worked with, who had given of himself to a young man new to the Metropolitan Police, and had become a friend.

I had not met Constable Martin, but I had heard him mentioned in conversations between Brodie and Mr. Dooley. A colorful story shared over a dram or cup of coffee in that way of mutual experiences had provided me another glimpse of the man I had married. And now his care and respect for Maddy Martin.

I let him have his silence and his thoughts.

"I thank ye, lass."

I looked back from window of the coach and the congestion on the street. That dark gaze softened as it met mine.

"For the care ye took with her, someone ye dinna know and beneath ye, as most would see it."

"She is quite extraordinary and so very strong," I replied.

"Aye, like yerself."

I shook my head. "I cannot imagine what she must feel. To have been married to her husband for so long, and now..."

"Ye canna imagine being with someone for over twenty years?"

I knew what he was thinking.

"I can," I replied, with no small amount of surprise at the thought. "As long as you don't get yourself killed. I would be very angry, Mr. Brodie."

The hazards of the inquiry business, still perhaps no more dangerous than that of a constable with the Metropolitan Police.

"Would ye now? No regrets?"

It was too tempting. And perhaps a little levity was called for.

"You do have a habit of leaving your clothes strewn about. And there is the matter of the toothpowder spilled all over the place."

"And ye have no odd habits?" he commented.

"Of course not," I replied somewhat cheekily. "But then, you knew that when you proposed to me."

There was a faint smile.

"A moment of insanity to be certain."

There was more silence and other thoughts.

"Will she be all right?" I inquired.

"Aye, in time, and with answers. It willna change any of it, but it will bring her some comfort."

"I was thinking..." I replied. "I would like very much to assist with the inquiries. It isn't as if I haven't in the past, and it's important… Food is one thing," I continued. "Perhaps assistance with the rents until she is able to decide what she will do next." I looked up and discovered him watching me.

"What is it?" I inquired.

He reached across the aisle of the coach and took my hand.

"Who could imagine a fine lady capable of shooting a criminal or runnin' 'em through with a sword having care for a constable's widow?"

"Do you know such a person?" I replied. His warm hand continued to hold mine.

"Or care for a man from the streets? And join yer life to his with a few words?" His fingers stroked the ring on my hand.

I could have told him that it was his heart that drew me to him. Or it might be his loyalty to a friend such as Constable Martin. And above all, there was the trust I had discovered when I had learned not to trust anyone.

"It was something Aunt Antonia recommended quite highly, as a matter of fact," I replied.

"What might that be?"

He could be such a devil. He knew perfectly well what I was speaking of, admittedly not quite the same as those other qualities, but equally impressive.

However, I was not about to give him the satisfaction of telling him. At least not specifically. I smiled to myself.

"It's your ability to build the 'perfect fire' in the coal stove on a cold winter's night," I replied.

He released my hand and sat back in the seat of the coach. A bit of the devil had returned to that dark gaze that watched me.

"Ye are indecent, Mikaela Forsythe. Speaking of such things in the middle of the day."

"I have no idea what you are speaking of."

He was thoughtful.

"Wot of yer meeting with Lady Ambersley earlier this morning?"

I had met with Kitty Ambersley at the request of Sir Laughton, my great-aunt's lawyer, in the matter of a missing necklace that had apparently disappeared from her London residence after a supper party.

The necklace was quite valuable, handed down through the Ambersley ancestors, and Kitty, as she was known to society friends, was quite beside herself at the loss of it.

She had reached out to my great-aunt with the hope that we might be able to assist in the recovery of the necklace that was said to be worth more than a half million pounds. The detachable brooch, with a diamond cluster surrounding a large blue diamond, was said to be extremely rare.

"Her husband is a member of Parliament and highly respected. She is...how should I say this?" Sir Laughton had attempted to explain. "Somewhat unconventional in her views."

He had been rather circumspect in his description.

"Perhaps even a bit eccentric.

"I realize that you and Brodie do not usually take on cases about stolen items," he continued. "However, it would be a favor to me, as well as your great-aunt, as they are well acquainted.

"Lady Ambersley is quite devastated at the loss and is hopeful you will consider making inquiries."

That was two weeks earlier.

I had discussed it with Brodie, and we agreed that we would make our usual inquiries from a list of staff, servants, and guests provided.

We had received that list the day before, and Sir Laughton had sent round word for Lady Ambersley to meet us at his office to discuss the situation. There, I had explained how we worked, the inquiries we would make on her behalf, yet warned that there was no guarantee that it would bring the recovery of the necklace.

To that end, I had also explained to her that the theft of such a valuable piece of jewelry might very well result in the necklace being either sold off to an unknown buyer or broken into smaller pieces and then sold. Such was the reality for items of value that were stolen, including jewels.

Brodie remained at the office this morning to take care of some correspondence regarding another inquiry about our services. And then, of course, the unexpected visit from Mr. Dooley.

Eccentric. A word that had often been used to describe my great-aunt. It was most certainly an understatement for Lady Ambersley—Kitty as she preferred that I call her.

For our meeting she had arrived at Sir Laughton's office wearing a brilliant purple gown with a purple satin coat over and a matching turban.

It was not the turban that was somewhat amusing. Aunt Antonia had been known to wear them from time to time. It was the small dog she carried that also wore matching purple satin.

"The dog's name is Bitsy. She would be no more than a mouthful for the hound," I added.

I then spoke of the meeting with Lady Ambersley that followed, although it seemed that Brodie was very likely not listening, considering the frown on his face and the lines between those dark brows.

I was not surprised. The news about Constable Martin's

death was dreadful, and admittedly a far more serious matter that Kitty Ambersley's dog.

"I explained how we usually proceed with an inquiry and also explained that the necklace might very well have been broken up and sold in pieces or smuggled out of the country."

He eventually looked up, the frown still there.

"Ye will be acquainted with most of the people on the list of names she provided. It might be best if ye were to make the necessary inquiries. I need to let Mr. Conner know about Constable Martin. They worked together for a number of years. And then I want to make inquiries among those I know."

"Of course. I would like to help," I added.

He looked at me. "I thank ye for the thought, lass." He shook his head. "It is somethin' I need to do and the places I need to go..."

I understood, I really did, and I knew that he had the experience to keep himself safe and was perfectly capable. Still...

"When will you begin?" I asked as we returned to the office.

He didn't reply, which told me that he already had. Perhaps in that conversation with Mr. Dooley.

"I will make the inquiries for Lady Ambersley." Although I was not looking forward to the appointment I had made for later that afternoon and wondered if Bitsy would still be wearing purple satin.

It might have been something in my voice.

"It's not that I dinna want yer help, but there are things here that..." Brodie started to explain.

"I understand. Hopefully this will be resolved quickly." I thought of Maddy Martin. "For everyone's sake."

He went into the adjacent room that served as our

bedroom whenever we were on a case and returned late at night, or in the event of dreadful weather.

The single room had been quite plain with only a bed and washstand when I first sought his inquiry service.

It had been expanded somewhat and now included a wardrobe for our clothes as well as a water closet.

My great-aunt had also seen to it that we had what she considered 'appropriate furnishings' for a professional office.

All in all, the office at #204 on the Strand had been transformed in no small part to her efforts.

"*Ye may do as ye see fit with the place, but dinna touch my desk,*" Brodie had told me at the time.

In addition to the expanded office and furnishings, we had decided to have a lift installed beside the alcove near the sidewalk, mostly for the ease of Mr. Cavendish, so he could access the second floor.

He had previously used a bell at the end of a rope near the landing to let us know that someone arrived or a message had been received. The loyal former soldier had been with Brodie since he first began offering his inquiry services. Mr. Cavendish had previously lived in the alcove at the bottom of the stairs along with the hound.

Rupert belonged to no one and usually occupied the alcove near the street when the weather turned. However, he and I got on quite well.

I had given the hound his name. He reminded me of the hunting dogs my father kept when I was a child, that included one in particular I was quite fond of, also named Rupert.

In spite of his habit of scrounging the streets for whatever dead creature might be found and bringing it back to the alcove, he had proven himself to be a stalwart friend and fierce protector on more than one occasion.

When Brodie emerged once more from the adjacent room, he was dressed in common worker's clothes—black woven-cotton trousers, a black jumper, and scuffed boots, instead of the fine worsted coat, shirt, and tie that he had worn earlier.

He might have been any drayman or cabman on the street, with overlong hair in need of a trim, full beard, and a billed cap.

"I will leave word for Mr. Dooley," he told me as he retrieved his jacket from the coat stand. "If he should return here, I want very much to see the police report that was made about the matter."

I was tempted to ask when he might return but did not.

He then went to his desk, opened the top drawer and retrieved the revolver he always carried when he went out on the street while on a case—old habits, he once explained.

"Leave a message with Mr. Cavendish if ye need to get word to me."

I nodded.

"And dinna go about alone after nightfall."

"I still would like to help," I said once more.

"Aye, but I need you here, and there is the Ambersley inquiry."

"You will be careful?" I added. "I would hate for something to happen to you and leave me with all of this."

He reached out and touched my cheek.

"Careful as church mice."

And then he was out the door, down the stairs, with a word to Mr. Cavendish, before disappearing among the crowd of carts and coaches on the street.

We had taken separate cases in the past. Still, I preferred when we worked together. I had learned a great deal from him. And admittedly he had learned a few things as well. Still...

As I was about to close the door, the hound appeared and slipped through the opening.

"Gave you the word, did he?" I commented.

The hound looked up at me with those large dark eyes, grinned, and then went to the coal stove and lay down on the rug before it.

"I thought so."

My appointment with Lady Ambersley to begin my interviews with servants was slated for later in the afternoon.

That would give me the opportunity to question servants as well as inspect the residence at St. John's Wood the way I had learned from Brodie.

I then went to the chalkboard and spent the next hour making my usual notes regarding the Ambersley inquiry, as well as the questions I wanted to ask.

When the clock struck one, I put my notebook in my travel bag, then donned my long coat.

"Come along then," I told Rupert. "You will stay here. I don't believe Bitsy would appreciate your handsome self."

At the sidewalk below the office, I asked Mr. Cavendish to wave down a coach.

"When might you return, miss?" he inquired, squinting up at me through the misty rain from under the bill of his cap.

It was as I thought. He rarely inquired about such things. It did seem as though Brodie had put out the word to him regarding my travels about London in his absence.

Once again, I was not surprised. I informed Mr. Cavendish that I would return to Mayfair after meeting with our client. It was quite near St. John's Wood.

"That would be before dark," he said as a reminder.

As I was saying...

BRODIE

"What have the lads at the MET done about it?" Mr. Conner inquired as he sat across from Brodie in his small flat in Holborn.

"They are makin' their usual inquiries," Brodie replied. "It was late at night as he finished his rounds, and no one was around that late of the hour in the Circus."

Conner made a crude sound. "Most of Abberline's people wouldn't know how to find themselves if they had a mirror. No criticism of Mr. Dooley, but he's just one man.

"And you know as well as meself that Abberline will fuss about it for a while and then it will be put aside for other matters as he has in the past. Ones that will look best on his record now that he's been reinstated."

Brodie wasn't surprised that Conner was aware of that.

"You know as well that there are few beside the lot of us who served with Constable Martin who care if the murderer is found—risks of the work and not a priority."

Brodie nodded. "I though ye would want to know."

Conner was thoughtful. "What of his widow? Was there any mention to her of someone he came across before that night? Some difficulty on the street?"

"Nothing that he told her."

Conner slammed down the empty glass that had held a good portion of whisky earlier.

"Now, tell me lad, what is it you plan to do?"

"I will start with his usual route, speak with workers that were in the area late in the day who might have seen someone lurking about, or heard something about it on the street."

"That is a lot for one man. It takes time, and you know the more time that passes, the less chance we have finding the bastard."

"Aye," Brodie replied.

"Two can cover the area in half the time."

"You haven't walked the street in over ten years," Brodie pointed out, instead of reminding Conner of his age and the remnants of old injuries that still plagued him from his own time in uniform.

"You forget, lad. I'm a Scot the same as yerself, and as long as there's a bit of the drink at the end of the day, I can still walk miles around you. Where do we begin?"

Brodie had known what his response would be, and the truth was that, having told him, he would be hard-pressed to prevent Conner from taking to the streets.

"We start at Regent Street. We'll split the route from here."

Conner poured another dram for them both.

"To warm the blood before we set off, and a toast to find the bloody bastard that murdered a good man."

Three

MIKAELA

THE RESIDENCE OF SIR AMBERSLEY, at St. John's Wood near Regent's Park, was an impressive Georgian red-brick manor, with ornate window bays set above a portico entrance.

I paid the coachman, then climbed the half dozen steps to the main entrance, where I was met by a footman in the usual livery of a servant in such an impressive residence.

What? Not dressed in vivid purple, I thought, somewhat sarcastically. I then heard the high-pitched yapping of an animal that could only be Bitsy as the alarm of my arrival was sounded.

"This way, Lady Forsythe," the footman indicated with what could only be described as a mixed expression of propriety for the position he held and what could only be described as forced tolerance.

I thought of the hound and silently sympathized.

"Good afternoon, Lady Forsythe," a servant who could

only be the head butler greeted me as Bitsy finally made an appearance, charging across the entrance hall like a bad hairpiece that had suddenly come to life. "I am Mr. Ives."

The introduction was interrupted by Bitsy as she made directly for me, obviously determined to guard the manor against intruders. She seized the hem of my coat and began to furiously chew on it.

I had a great fondness for animals, case in point the hound. Unruly behavior was undoubtedly not this poor creature's fault. However, I was not one to stand idly by while an overgrown rat proceeded to ruin my coat.

"Stop!" I firmly admonished.

It was undoubtedly the first time, the word—spoken somewhat firmly—had ever been uttered.

Quite startled, Bitsy ceased her gnawing, sprang back in a mass of quivering incredulity, and stared at me through a curtain of perfectly groomed bangs.

Mr. Ives promptly coughed, no doubt to disguise his surprise as well, a bemused expression at his face.

"If you will come this way, Lady Forsythe. Lady Ambersley will join you in the drawing room forthwith."

And *forthwith*, Bitsy followed, at a curious but cautious distance.

It was perhaps best that Brodie had not accompanied me. He might have been tempted to shoot the poor thing.

Afternoon tea was provided as Kitty Ambersley made her appearance, dressed in fuchsia, turban included. It did seem that she had a penchant for vivid color, including the bright shade on her cheeks. She smiled in greeting as I reminded myself of the most serious reason I was there.

"I do hope that Bitsy has been entertaining you."

Entertaining was such an interesting word.

"Most entertaining," I replied as she scooped the destructive little creature into her arms and proceeded to kiss her.

"She is most protective..." she explained.

Of course, I thought. Any intruder or attacker would be absolutely terrified.

"And can be very forceful when needed"

As in, destroying the hem of one's coat? I smiled.

"Shall we begin?" I replied.

I had several questions for Lady Ambersley:

When did she last have the necklace?

Did she keep it in a particular place when not wearing it? A wall safe perhaps?

Had she returned it that night after the supper party? Or perhaps mislaid it?

"I wore it the night of the supper party."

"It's usually kept in a box in my wardrobe." A place where anyone might have access to it.

"I remember laying it atop my dressing table before I dressed for bed." Not helpful there.

"And you will want to speak with the servants," she had added then.

"Yes, if you will be kind enough to let me see your private rooms," I added.

"I have explained that I laid it on my dressing table. It's not there now. It has disappeared."

My smile was painful. I explained that it could be useful to see the place she spoke of and perhaps find a clue what might have happened to the necklace.

"Oh, I do see. This is so exciting. To think there might have been a thief here."

I was not inclined to think that it was exciting that a thief was there. I smiled again.

"If you would be so kind as to show me your private rooms?" I reminded her for a place to begin.

"Of course."

She set dear Bitsy on the floor. The animal assumed a safe distance as Kitty Ambersley escorted me to her private rooms.

I had developed a throbbing headache.

There was nothing unusual discovered in the search of Lady Ambersley's private rooms.

Other than the fact that she was in the habit of leaving a trail of clothes about the rooms, all either in a shade of purple or fuchsia, including a purple wig on a wood head stand in her private dressing chamber. And there were those who thought my great-aunt was eccentric!

I wondered if Sir Ambersley was similarly kitted out. That conjured up amusing images and would most certainly make the meetings at Parliament most interesting.

We had then returned to the formal drawing room where late afternoon tea was served, including scones filled with dried fruit and nuts. Rupert would have been ecstatic, as scones were a favorite treat.

Not that I was above slipping a bit of the crumbly delight to the current animal who had followed my every move, at a safe distance, when Kitty Ambersley went to request the guest list from the night of the supper party.

Bitsy tentatively took the bit of scone, then stepped back a safe distance once more. It appeared we had an understanding.

With the list in hand, I thanked Kitty Ambersley and explained that I would be calling on the guests from that night if she would be so good as to contact them in the matter.

It was after five o'clock when I left the Ambersley manor,

darkness settling over St. John's Wood, with the lights of Regent's Park glowing through the misty rain.

Lady Ambersley had Mr. Ives summon their driver for the short ride to Mayfair.

I fully expected the coach to be decorated in purple wool, stained purple leather, and window shades, and was surprised that it was not.

Surprisingly, my headache had all but disappeared by the time I arrived at the townhouse.

My housekeeper, Mrs. Ryan, had prepared supper. A warm fire burned on the hearth in the front parlor.

After removing my coat, I went into the parlor and poured myself a dram of Old Lodge whisky.

It was all quite cozy—that was the word for it. The whisky was most excellent.

I went to my writing desk and retrieved my notebook from my travel bag to set down my notes from the afternoon meeting with Lady Kitty Ambersley.

Yet there was something missing...

BRODIE

The shopkeeper at Mellins Food shop shook his head.

"I heard about it. Sad bit of news. Didn't notice anything unusual. Constable Martin was well thought of around here, with a new partner that was learning the ways of the street. Seemed like a nice young chap.

"We felt safe with Constable Martin about. When he was on early patrol, he would purchase food from me shop to take home to the missus.

"It won't be the same. They'll send some other bloke out, but he won't have the same way with those about the Circus."

"Aye, no one saw anything unusual," Conner muttered as they met later at the end of Regent Street. "I also checked with city transportation dispatch the next street over. There's no record of any driver that pulled a late-night fare around the time Dooley claims that Joe's partner found him on Regent Street."

Brodie nodded. It was a familiar answer for both men.

"I'll have a word with old Mick and Rafferty. They may be done with the MET as well, but they hear things. Mick will be at a pub by this time, and Rafferty..." His voice trailed off.

"He can usually be found with a certain woman." There was a grin. "Not that I would be interruptin' anything. He's been complainin' about 'things' not wot they once were, if ye get my meanin'."

He did. There had been a conversation or two about that in the past.

"Not that I suppose ye have any difficulty of that nature," Conner added.

Brodie let that pass.

The congestion at the thoroughfare gradually eased, and the lights along Piccadilly Circus lit up the darkening sky.

Conner rubbed his hands together against the cold that came with the misty rain that had begun.

Brodie noticed the gesture as well as the stiffness in the man's gait as they met once more on the street, remnants from too many years spent walking the patrol as they had the past hours.

"See wot Mick and Rafferty might know. Leave word with Mr. Cavendish if ye learn something," Brodie replied. "I'll see wot others may have heard on the street. There's usually something to be learned when a man with the MET goes down."

"Mr. Brown?" Conner inquired.

Brodie nodded.

"Watch yer back, lad. Ye might no longer be with the MET, but ye are well known among those who wear the uniform. Have a care for some yob out to make a name for himself."

Brodie nodded. There was a time in the past when he had been called that, among other things, in his time on the street.

They parted, Conner for the pub where he could find a pint and a conversation with old Mick. Rafferty had retired out with an injury just after Brodie joined the service, and he had not known him well.

There had been talk...there was always talk. It seemed that the old Irishman might have been on the take with one of the street gangs. He did seem to live far more comfortably than others in the uniform. Making a bit of money on the side. It was not unusual with a man's usual pay of twenty-five shillings sixpence weekly. Half usually went for rent of a small flat, that left little over for food or other necessities.

Brodie had shared a flat with Munro for a time, though he was rarely there but working some enterprise on the streets. He didn't inquire wot those enterprises might have been, though he heard rumors on the street.

His pay increased to three pounds fourteen shillings when he made inspector, then four pounds and eight weekly by the time he left.

Brodie turned up his collar as he waved down a cab and set off for his meeting with Algernon Brown at Bethnal Green, where he operated out of a tavern near the brewery.

Not that the man used his given name, as Brodie had

learned in his time with the MET. On the street he was simply known as *Mr. Brown*, along with a dangerous reputation.

"And I'll thank you not to use the name," Brown had once told him. "It's not good for business."

Brodie understood, considering the man's business—graft, extortion, smuggling among those who would cut a man's throat just for lookin' at him wrong. The name didn't command fear or respect.

It was well into the night when the cabman delivered him to the edge of Bethnal Green. From there, he walked the familiar slums, doss houses, and poor tenements, with a watchful eye to the shadows.

He knew the area well, although the MET rarely patrolled this part of London because of the crime and high murder rate, where a man could easily disappear in a quarrel over a coin and never be seen again.

And the women were often as bad, or worse, than the men. It was nothing for a man to be found in a room in a tenement house with his throat cut or floating in the river when he refused to pay for his time with one of the prostitutes that worked the area.

A sudden movement caught his attention as a man came at him out of those shadows.

His attacker was equally tall and stout, the fumes from a local pub thick in the air as he attacked and caught Brodie on the near side. Quick and experienced, the man brought up a blade.

He caught his attacker by the arm, twisted it and brought it up at a sharp angle at the man's back.

"Ye dinna want to do this," he snarled at him. "Drop the blade."

The man continued to struggle. "There are others," his

attacker growled. "Ye'll not get away!"

"I dinna want to get away. Now, drop the blade and tell me who the devil are ye, before I snap yer arm from yer shoulder?"

The man refused to answer, and Brodie yanked his arm higher. He let out a howl, then spit out a string of oaths.

"The blade!" Brodie reminded him. It clattered to the stones beside the building.

"Wot are ye called?" he demanded again.

"Me arm!" the man screamed.

"I'll break it off and beat ye with it. Yer name!" Brodie again demanded as he kicked the man's feet and knocked him off balance, then spun him around and slammed him against the side of a tenement house.

"Murphy!" the man cried out, a garbled, muffled sound against the crumbling stones on the wall of the house.

"Jasper Murphy?"

There was a grudging nod as the man continued to buck against his hold.

Brodie shoved him hard against that wall, the stone darkening with blood in the flickering light from a lantern in the window above the street.

He wrestled the man around and slammed him once more against the side of the building as he brought up the revolver and pressed the tip of the barrel to the side of the man's head.

He knew the name.

"If ye move wrong, if ye so much as twitch, there will be a bullet in yer head. Now, come along and we will call on the man ye work for."

It was not far. The question was, had Murphy simply made a mistake, or had he been sent.

He dragged Murphy by the neck of his coat, pulled him

back to his feet when he stumbled, then dragged him the rest of the way to the tavern.

When they reached the entrance, he pulled Murphy with him through the opening into the glare of light, the stench of bodies, and the cacophony of rowdy conversation with crude curses. He shoved Murphy before him, rolling him across the stained wood floor in a tangled heap of bruises and bloodied flesh.

"I'm here to see Mr. Brown," he announced, the revolver held at the ready by his side.

"Ye can tell him that I am here for our meetin'."

"It's dangerous to go into certain places," a gruff voice replied. "It could get a man killed."

Brodie nodded. "Aye, it could."

Four

BRODIE

"YOU LIVE DANGEROUSLY, MY FRIEND. COMIN' here and takin' on one of my men the way he claimed," Brown commented as he and Brodie sat across from each other with a pint at a table in the tavern.

"Our encounter was a bit different than he spoke of," Brodie corrected his account of the situation.

"He's thick in the head," Brown replied. "But good when there's a need for muscle. Now tell me, what brings ye here, before any more of my people end up bloodied."

Brodie explained about the attack and death of his friend.

Brown nodded. "I remember the man. He was always fair, even looked the other way in a couple of encounters in the past, and now you want to find the killer. Were there witnesses?"

"I would not be here if there were."

Brown nodded with understanding. "I've always thought that you would make a fine addition to my 'business.' You know the streets and your way around them and the people in them, including the bloody peelers. And now you want my help."

It was not the first time Brown had made the offer.

"Work? For ye?"

"It never hurts to ask. But I do understand with your arrangement with Lady Forsythe that you might be reluctant, and truth be known, I don't blame ye. I might give all of this up for one such as her."

Brodie nodded. "I need information, more eyes and ears on the street. It's no secret that you have the largest number of 'associates' working for ye. And ye know as well that the murder of a constable is not something that remains secret."

Brown agreed. "The truth of it is, that it's like a medal some like to wear." He sat back in his chair.

"I owe you for letting me know about Abberline's secret campaign to make a sweep of known places where my people work, now that he's returned. Out to make amends with the Home Secretary for certain, after that bit of disgrace that nearly got you killed. Are you certain you won't join my band of merry thieves?"

"Certain. I would not want to offend the lady either."

Brown threw back his head and roared with laughter. "She is a formidable woman, and deadly with a revolver from what I hear—gives as good as she gets."

As Brodie knew only too well, nothing ever remained secret. Not even a previous case that had involved the royal family.

"Tell me who you've questioned, the reputable people of business, no doubt. I'll put the word out to *my* people," Brown replied. "That will square us then."

Brodie smiled. "Until you need information from me."

He remained for another round and told Brown whom

he'd spoken with, including Maddy Martin, and also told him that Mr. Conner was making similar inquiries.

"And what of your partner in crime? Munro?"

He didn't take offense. Munro's endeavors from the past were known to those who needed to know, as were his own.

"Aye," he acknowledged.

Brown nodded as Brodie stood to leave after placing several coins on the table.

"Just so that I dinna owe for the beer."

"That's what I like about you, Brodie. You always 'leave the table square,' not like others I know."

The man's meaning was not lost on him, a lesson he learned early on—*leave the table square* so that he owed nothing to anyone. When dealing with people like Brown, it was a good way to stay alive.

"I'll be on the street as well," he told Brown so there would not be another encounter like this evening. "Leave word with Mr. Cavendish if ye learn something," he added as he stood to leave.

Brown snorted. "That crippled old seadog?"

"That seadog works for me, and he can be trusted."

He didn't mention the hound. Let Brown's people learn that lesson if they threatened Cavendish.

When he left the tavern, he was aware of the shadows that followed at a distance as he left Bethnal Green.

MIKAELA, #204 THE STRAND

I left Mayfair early.

Brodie had not returned the night before.

While I had hoped that he would so that I might learn if he had been able to obtain any information about the murder of Constable Martin, I was well aware that questioning people was tedious work and often looked upon with suspicion. Most particularly when someone had been murdered, as I had learned in the past.

There were those who knew nothing, those who might cooperate with some bit of information, and those who would refuse to provide any information, particularly with the murderer still out there somewhere.

The weather had hardly improved over the day before, the roadway awash with flotsam that included remnants of garbage, soggy day-old newspapers, and the usual clogged traffic as carts and coaches slowly proceeded, then abruptly stopped, until I was convinced it would have been far quicker afoot.

However, the driver cautioned me against it.

"You don't want to be out and about in this," he said as I inquired if another route might be more expedient.

He shook his head. "It's worse on the side streets. Best to keep to the main roadway."

The flooding was not an unusual occurrence after a heavy rain. At least the Strand was far enough from the river that we didn't have bodies washing up on the sidewalks.

I took out my notebook and read back over the notes I had made the previous day.

I'd learned of nothing suspicious while questioning the servants during my initial visit, nor my inspection of the servant's quarter or the Ambersley private rooms.

All of the servants were long-time members of the Ambersley staff, although I knew well enough that a change in one's personal circumstances might provide a motive. Still, there was not a servant recently replaced, nor had one left suddenly over some complaint.

Kitty Ambersley had provided a list of her dinner guests from the night of the supper party. It had been a small affair with only two gentlemen and their wives joining them.

I was doubtful there would be any help there, as both guests were well-placed and known to be quite wealthy as well. In spite of the value of the necklace, it did seem that neither one or the other had a need to take to thievery. They could well afford to purchase such an item for themselves.

Still, it was important to 'turn over every stone' in the effort to learn what had happened to the necklace.

I had discovered that one never knew the true nature of a person that might be hidden from others. And I was determined to see the matter through by taking the usual steps in an inquiry case.

I had placed telephone calls from the townhouse to the residence of Lord Anthony Longridge as well as Sir William Atherton before leaving and requested a meeting with each of the ladies regarding that evening.

I had an appointment with Lady Longridge later this morning, and another with Lady Atherton in the early afternoon.

We eventually arrived at the office on the Strand without mishap. I paid the driver as Mr. Cavendish navigated the sidewalk and greeted me.

"Thought you might choose to stay at the townhouse with this nasty bit of flooding. That was a downpour last night, and it seems the city people in their fine offices have a problem with the street backing up all the way to the park. The hound had to swim across earlier."

No doubt a bit of an exaggeration, yet there were still

several inches of water washing against the curb at the street. A frequent occurrence in the midst of winter in spite of the sewer system that was celebrated to have solved the flooding from the Thames.

"I hope you were not washed out of the alcove," I told Mr. Cavendish. It could have been very difficult him to navigate several inches of water.

"Not at all, miss. As the weather set in, me and the hound set off for the Public House, then to the flat after."

The flat was a new accommodation for him after his marriage in December to Miss Effie, who worked at the Public House. She had moved to a ground-floor flat that came available prior to the wedding and prevailed upon the building owner to install a ramp for Mr. Cavendish's use. The flat was very near the office.

"Though the hound wasn't too keen on remaining the night. He was pacing the place, so Effie let him out. The animal does prefer the street."

Said animal had emerged from the alcove that was part of the building and usually remained relatively dry during weather. Relative, that is, considering Rupert's comings and goings.

He had started up the stairs then stopped midway and appeared to be waiting for me to follow.

"Did Mr. Brodie return last night?" I inquired of Mr. Cavendish.

"Not before I set out for the Public House, miss."

I thanked him and would have taken the lift, recently installed for ease of reaching the second and third floors of the building. We were progressing into the modern era in spite of Brodie's insistence that it was not necessary—the lift that is.

However, Rupert was quite insistent, returning to the base of the stairs, tail wagging furiously, and barking insistently.

"Oh, very well," I told him, something that Brodie found quite amusing—talking to Rupert as if he was capable of understanding. I was working on that, as I knew perfectly well that he understood most everything I said.

Rupert turned and charged up the stairs. I gathered my skirts and followed. I suddenly stopped at the landing.

He had nosed his way into the office!

He was extremely smart as I had discovered in the past, yet I was fairly certain that unlocking the office door was not among his many talents. Which of course raised the question, how had it become unlocked?

He now stood in the middle of the office and barked most insistently. I cautiously pushed the door fully open. As I did, Rupert began to inspect the office, nose to the floor, obviously tracking a scent. His inspection took him into the adjacent flat, where he let out another bark.

He emerged, head cocked, ears up, and barked again, inspection apparently concluded. At least to assure me that there was no one lurking about.

"Good boy," I told him as I slowly walked into the office and began my own inspection that included the remnants of damp footprints on the carpet, apparently left by whoever had been there.

Was it possible that Brodie had returned in the middle of the night?

It seemed logical that he might have, since he was out and about in all sorts of places, quite determined to learn more about Constable Martin's murder.

I carefully continued my inspection as Rupert returned to the office and sat expectantly before the coal stove.

The chalkboard appeared to be as I had left it the previous day, with the felt eraser in the same place on the chalk rail.

The file on Brodie's desk that he had been working on, adding notes from our last case, was on the corner of his desk, although upon closer inspection it did seem as if it might have been moved. I then went to my desk.

Brodie insisted that I have my own desk and had gifted me with a portable typing machine. Even though he had insisted at the time that it might be useful when working on my next novel.

I was not fooled that it also just happened to be most convenient for typing out our case reports. His handwriting was often indecipherable. There were moments when he was quite transparent.

Instead of inquiring if I would type the report, he had grumbled and groused that he couldn't read the "damned thing," tossing the folder back down onto the desk with obvious impatience.

How had I responded when I usually would not have patience for such things?

"Let me type up the report, dear, rather than listen to your complaints and curses."

It was not lost on me, by the self-satisfied smirk on his face, that he had maneuvered the situation to his favor. Yet, I had discovered there were ways to get back at him.

I straightened the folder and noticed that the edge was damp as if something had spilled on it. I opened it. The top page of the report was faintly smudged, as if whoever had opened the folder had smudged the ink on the page. I closed the file.

Rupert had joined my inspection and sat expectantly with that same demeanor as moments before.

"What is it? What do you think you've found?" I went to my desk.

Everything seemed in order—pencil holder, a tablet for notes when Brodie and I discussed a case, a copy of my last novel that James Warren, my publisher and also my brother-in-law, had sent to the office just before the volume's recent release at the bookstores.

I frowned. I was almost certain that I had placed it on the bookshelf with other books I had brought to the office. As I reached for it to return it to the shelf, I noticed drops of what appeared to be water on the desktop. I glanced at the door that had been ajar when I arrived. From what I had discovered, it did seem that someone had been in the office.

Brodie would not have left the office unlocked and the door ajar.

Rupert nudged my hand. I stroked his ears. I had no doubt that he sensed...something. Or someone.

"It does seem as though we had a visitor," I commented, not that I expected a response.

And it did appear that it was not Brodie. While he was very supportive of my efforts as an author, he had yet to read one of my Emma Fortescue novels, especially with her recent adventures in crime solving.

"I'm afraid wot I might find that ye've written there. Particularly how women gather about when ye have a new book out."

Dear Emma, the heroine of my novels, had taken on a partner in her endeavors—a tall, dark, brooding Scot! I had yet to make Rupert a central character.

He whined at my feet.

"Good boy," I commended him. At least he hadn't dropped a body part or some dead creature at my feet.

I crossed the office and checked the lock. It worked quite well, yet I did notice scratch marks about the keyhole.

We kept nothing of value there other than the few furnishings, my typing machine, and extra clothes for those days that went long into the night when on a case. Yet, someone had gone to considerable effort to get into the office.

What had they hoped to find?

I made a mental note to have Mr. Cavendish send word to the locksmith that we needed the lock changed and new keys provided, then removed my neck scarf and coat.

There was time before my first appointment, and I wanted to update my notes regarding the Ambersley lost necklace. I paused as I went to the chalkboard.

It was safe to assume that whoever had been there had also seen my notes. There was nothing to indicate that it was connected to the case of the lost necklace. Still...

I decided to update my notebook instead. While it was an extremely remote possibility that whoever had been there was connected to the loss of the necklace, I was not one to take chances. It was a very valuable piece of jewelry.

Instead, I sat at Brodie's desk and updated my notebook. I then wrote a note for when he returned to the office that I would give to Mr. Cavendish.

With the dreadful weather, I left extra time for travel to my first appointment. As the clock struck the hour ahead of our meeting time, I gathered my notebook and retrieved my scarf and coat. I made certain that I locked the door as I left the office.

Mr. Cavendish was there as Rupert and I reached the sidewalk. I handed him the note for Brodie.

"Please see that he receives this when he returns," I asked, then waved down a coach.

"Is everything all right, miss?"

"It does seem as though someone visited the office last night."

He cut a glance to the top of the stairs. "Mr. Brodie perhaps?"

I shook my head. "The lock had been tampered with. Please contact the locksmith to change the lock."

He nodded as a coach arrived with Mr. Jarvis, who frequently provided transportation, atop with his cap pulled low against the rain.

"Will the lad be accompanying you?" he inquired with a look down at the hound.

"It would be best, with what you just told me," Mr. Cavendish suggested.

"He's better mannered than some of me fares," Mr. Jarvis added.

It did seem that the matter had already been decided.

"Very well," I replied.

"Up with you," I told Rupert.

He scrambled into the coach. I gave Mr. Jarvis the address for my meeting with Lady Longridge and then climbed in after.

Five

MY APPOINTMENT with Lady Longridge was pleasant.

I had asked Mr. Jarvis to wait. Rupert presented a different problem.

"No worry, miss," Mr. Jarvis assured me. "The lad can stay with me. We get along right fine."

That, of course, was always subject to Rupert's mood at the moment, not to mention his appetite that often took him off on adventures. Yet, Mr. Cavendish had assured me that he'd had a fine meal earlier, courtesy of Miss Effie at the Public House.

Unfortunately, as I had anticipated, my meeting with Lady Longridge brought no new revelations in the matter of the missing necklace. Yes, she remembered that Lady Ambersley had been wearing it, but there was some mishap with the clasp during a course of soup, and the necklace had dropped into her bowl.

Something that Lady Ambersley neglected to mention, although at the moment that didn't seem cause for alarm. It appeared that said necklace had then been wrapped in a cloth napkin to be duly cleaned after supper.

Mr. Jarvis and Rupert then escorted me to my afternoon meeting with Lady Atherton. The residence was nearer St. James's, and once again I left Rupert with Mr. Jarvis, although with some trepidation.

The property surrounding the Georgian manor was filled with trees, said trees filled with birds and undoubtedly a squirrel or two. Rupert did have a particular taste for squirrel, although a bird would do. He was most proficient at hunting both.

"I'll keep an eye on him, miss. I have a bit of sandwich in me pocket that should do the lad."

The 'lad' in question grinned at me. Never a good sign where food was involved.

Lady Atherton was somewhat older, of an age closer to that of my great-aunt, with various ailments that were not typical of my great-aunt.

"I do remember the incident with the necklace, yet it all seemed straight-forward. Lady Ambersley wrapped it in her dinner napkin and set it aside, and we carried on with supper."

There was a common memory of the evening. I supposed that it was possible that the necklace had been cleaned by a servant and then returned to Lady Ambersley. Or there was always the possibility that it was still wrapped in the dinner napkin and now amongst the laundry. It would require another visit with her.

I thanked Lady Atherton and returned to the coach, greeted by Mr. Jarvis with Rupert nowhere in sight.

"He needed a bit of airing off a short while ago, if ye get my meanin'. He should be back any time now."

I did understand his meaning. However, his confidence in Rupert's imminent return was open to doubt.

I called for him in the usual manner, then gave a loud whistle which did draw the attention of an elderly gentleman who passed in his coach.

Not one to stand on formality, I ignored the disapproving glare he gave me and whistled again.

Rupert soon appeared and I could only stare at the creature that dangled from his mouth. And still very much alive.

Traveling about with the hound had presented unique experiences in the past. At least this particular quarry was not bleeding.

I had been working with him in the past on a few commands, with varying success. Varying, as it did depend on his temperament of the moment if he chose to obey.

The commands were few, remembered from my childhood when my father had hunting dogs that included the first 'Rupert.' And then it was always questionable how this particular Rupert would react to a command.

"Give," I told him in a firm voice, the usual command to release what a hound had in its mouth.

He cocked his head to the side, the poor squirrel struggling to free itself. I could only imagine Lady Atherton emerging and possibly fainting dead away at having a squirrel torn to pieces in the portico.

"If you do not release the poor thing, I will be forced to cut off all sponge cake."

It was a thought, spoken in frustration, nothing more. Yet, Rupert promptly released the squirrel, which scampered off and then up the nearest tree.

Never underestimate the power of sponge cake, I thought, as Mr. Jarvis stared at me.

I ignored the obvious question and asked him to take me to Sussex Square. A conversation with my great-aunt was in order, as she undoubtedly knew both of the ladies I had spoken with.

I did have another reason for calling on her as well.

"Good afternoon, Lady Forsythe," Mr. Symons, my great-aunt's head butler, greeted me as I arrived at Sussex Square.

"Good afternoon. Is my great-aunt available? I didn't call before setting out."

"She is presently in the sword room with Miss Lily. I will have Jensen let her know of your arrival."

I thanked him.

"Not necessary. I know the way," I added and gave my coat and bag to the footman.

The sword room. Oh dear.

That conjured up visions of my aunt and Lily in full costume, swords drawn—blunted hopefully—and squaring off with one another. A situation fraught with frightening possibilities.

Aunt Antonia had given me lessons several years earlier, before I acquired professional lessons in Paris. And she was still strong and quite agile...for one who was near eighty-seven years of age. My concern was for Lily.

She was young, daring, and adventuresome to be certain, and with a bravado that might be considered reckless. I had visions of her attempting to outmaneuver my aunt, which might result in injury.

It was undoubtedly that protective instinct that Brodie had cautioned me about.

"Lady Montgomery has lived a long and most interesting life. And ye are the same—stubborn, too brave fer yer own good, and fierce when it comes to yer own. There is every possibility that she will outlive ye in spite of it all. Ye shouldn't worry yerself."

Yes, well. Far more easily said than done.

I took the staircase that led from the main floor to the second-floor chambers that included the sword room, then quickly traversed the long hall past other rooms, including my former bedchamber as well as my sister Linnie's.

That also included the portrait room with all those rather colorful ancestors glaring down from gilt frames, and Aunt Antonia's suite of rooms.

The portrait of our most notable ancestor, King William I, also known as William the Conqueror, was in the old part of Sussex Square, that was also referred to as the 'fortress.'

He had been an austere fellow, obviously not at all pleased to sit for a portrait, considering the expression on his face. Or he was possibly suffering from gout or some other malady.

I did have a rather colorful ancestry.

The sounds reached me before I came to the entrance to the sword room. There was a curse in a voice I easily recognized, followed by a ballyhoo.

"Aha! Now I have you."

I took a deep breath and prepared myself for mayhem, then entered the sword room, half expecting to see blood drawn.

Not precisely blood drawn, but the victor standing off her opponent with the tip of the rapier

"Oh, hello, dear. Do come in." Aunt Antonia greeted me as she stood over Lily, who was sprawled on the carpet, cheeks quite colorful from her exertions. Or possibly a tad of embarrassment at having apparently been bested by an opponent four times her age.

"We were just having a go at it. Lily was curious about a certain move."

"Are you all right?" I inquired, as my aunt stood back with a self-satisfied expression, and I extended a hand to Lily.

"Yes, very much so," she replied, as she took my offered hand, and I helped her to her feet.

"The woman is dangerous!" she whispered in a side comment.

"She is competitive. Always has been," I replied.

"I'm surprised that ye survived yer lessons with her."

"Hmmm, yes, she was a bit younger and quite..." I searched for the word. *Competitive* came to mind.

"You must remember that she is descended from fierce ancestors," I reminded her. "Including a highwayman or two, a duke who was known for the number of opponents he bested, and several others of somewhat dubious character and skill with both a blade and pistol. And she cannot be trusted to follow the rules," I added.

Lily grinned. "As I have learned. She is quite marvelous, isn't she?"

"Yes, she is."

"What brings you to Sussex Square, dear?" Aunt Antonia inquired as she removed her mask and tucked it under one arm. "Have I forgotten an engagement?"

"Not at all. I've taken an inquiry case for Lady Katherine Ambersley and have questions that I thought you might assist with."

"Kitty Ambersley?"

"The same."

"Let me change out of my costume, and I will join you in the small drawing room." She reached out and gently cupped Lily's chin.

"Are you quite all right, dear?"

Lily assured her that she was.

"I will be more aware of yer feint next time."

"I am warned," Aunt Antonia replied as she set off for her private chambers.

"Brodie is not with you?" she asked as I joined her in the small drawing room with Lily.

"Hmmm, no," I replied. "He is making inquiries in another matter."

She was quite fond of him

"Of course. Now, do tell me, what is this business with Kitty Ambersley?"

I explained what there was to know about the inquiries I was making, which was not a great amount of information.

"That damned necklace," my aunt commented as she poured us a dram of whisky. "You must know that it is not the first time the thing has gone missing."

"It has happened before?"

"Oh my, yes. Twice that I can think of. She eventually found it in the bodice of a gown she had been wearing, as I remember it. The second time, it was found by a servant in a bowl of gin punch at a holiday celebration. She is quite fond of gin," she added with a sniff of disapproval.

"I have never been able to understand that preference when there is excellent whisky available. She insists that it is a man's drink," she added as she raised her glass in a toast.

"I suppose Sir Ambersley tolerates her ridiculous habits due to her family being very well off and he a lawyer, although quite successful, I hear."

"Is she perhaps a bit…" I searched for the right word in an attempt to gain a better understanding of Lady Ambersley.

"*Eccentric* is the word," Aunt Antonia replied. "She does seem a bit odd. And then there is the dog. Very much an overgrown rat, but the woman is completely taken with the creature. Vile, yapping animal. Not like dear Rupert."

She was undoubtedly referring to Bitsy, which I would agree could hardly be considered to be a dog.

"The nasty little thing has been known to lift all sorts of things from those who call on Kitty. One has to beware not to set anything down."

Most interesting, I thought. In the absence of anything substantial in the way of clues and this latest piece of information, it did seem as if another visit with Kitty Ambersley was called for before I went any further on her behalf.

Not that I had anything against someone with a few eccentricities, Bitsy in this case, along with a few other things. After all, there were those who considered my great-aunt to be somewhat eccentric.

If they could only have seen her in the sword room earlier. I did adore her.

As for Lily, she was going to have to be more observant of those 'feint' tactics the next time she and Aunt Antonia took up the blades.

My great-aunt did have a great deal more experience in such things, and it was foolhardy to assume that someone of her mature age could not possibly be dangerous.

"You must stay for supper and tell us what Brodie is about with this other new case," she said as she called for the footman to inform Cook that I would be staying.

That would also give me the opportunity to speak with

Munro, as I was fairly certain he would know where Brodie was.

"Munro is not here," Lily informed me when I indicated that I wanted to speak with him.

"He took himself off early this morning," Aunt Antonia added. She gave me a knowing smile.

"It was some matter about a shipment from Old Lodge that needed attention."

Not that she was fooled for a moment. Nor was I.

It was a familiar excuse when Munro was off seeing to some other matter that he chose not to discuss. That other matter being Brodie, a fellow Scot, who was also his very good friend.

After supper, my great-aunt provided her driver, Mr. Hastings.

"Do be careful of Bitsy," she said in parting. "The creature can be quite a nuisance."

I'd already had experience with that. The thought did occur that I might take Rupert with me when next I met with Kitty Ambersley. He did have a particular preference for small furry creatures. Although that might be somewhat off-putting for Kitty Ambersley.

BRODIE

He slipped a coin across the table to the man who sat across from him, a man with knowledge of the streets who had been a source more than once in his time with the MET.

Sir Bartholemew was the name he went by, an affectation that spoke of his scorn for members of the ton, which included a habit of relieving them of their purses. A master pickpocket who had his portion of encounters with members of the constabulary, including Brodie.

Petty thievery, until he decided to 'up his game,' as it was called, and had relieved several well-heeled nobs in their coaches, which earned him the reputation as the 'thief of St. James's,' years earlier, when Brodie first made inspector.

Brodie had set a trap, once he figured out the man's usual scheme of waiting outside the residence of one of London's wealthier clients while posing as one of their own with the MET.

A stop, as a courtesy, to warn the passenger of trouble in the area, and the man or woman was relieved of their coin and valuables. An enterprising scheme, until it wasn't.

Once his scheme was discovered it was simply a matter of setting up a situation of a 'wealthy passenger,' leaving a St. James townhouse, and springing the trap.

Sir Bart, as he was known among his fellow thieves, had been more than surprised to find Brodie in the coach he stopped.

He had roared with laughter at the scheme that had put an end, at least temporarily, to his endeavors.

"It would take a thief to catch a thief!" he had exclaimed at the time, having met Brodie in a previous encounter before he joined the Met.

"I consider it a compliment, sir."

Sir Bart had served a sentence of three years and was then released, having claimed that he'd had a visitation from God and changed his ways.

A new scheme for the schemer.

The next time Brodie encountered him was in a matter of a theft from Mikaela's great-aunt, Lady Antonia Montgomery, after he had left the MET and worked for her in private inquiries.

"The old girl won't miss a few bottles of whisky," Sir Bart had pled the excuse when caught. "And you owe me for my time in Newgate."

"A fate of yer own makin'," Brodie had replied, then levelled a revolver at Sir Bart.

"Lady Montgomery is a client. I'll not have ye stealin' from her. But the choice is yers."

There had been some additional conversation after that, but in the end Sir Bart had decided that a bullet was perhaps not in his best interest.

As for wot Brodie owed him, he was not above keepin' a man in his back pocket, as the sayin' went.

It was always a good policy, particularly in the inquiry business, to have certain people he could rely on for information in exchange for an occasional favor, as in putting the word out to Sir Bart, with his new business enterprise, that certain people were looking for him.

Sir Bart scooped up the gold sovereign.

"Business must be good. And then there is that nice piece I heard ye got yerself married to."

Brodie ignored that, for the moment. He took out another coin and laid it in front of himself at the table.

"Wot do ye hear about the murder of Constable Martin?"

"A friend of yours, as I recall," Sir Bart commented with his usual affectation in keeping with that borrowed name.

Brodie nodded.

"It does seem odd that a man with his experience would become a victim." 'Sir Bart' sat back in his chair, his gaze flickering down to the coin.

"It could have merely been a common street person," he

speculated. "It does happen. Or is it possible that he knew the person?"

A thief's perspective. Brodie had the same thought.

Someone Martin knew? Who also knew his patrol route, and that he and his partner usually split the last walk around for the night?

Brodie retrieved the coin and pocketed it. The man hadn't told him anythin' he didn't already know or suspected.

"Or it might be someone with a score to settle," Sir Bart suggested. "There's a man by the name of Josephson who was let out not long ago."

The name wasn't familiar to him. But it might have been familiar to Constable Martin.

He took out the coin back out and shoved it across the table to Sir Bart.

"If ye hear something more, there will be more coin in it. Get word to Mr. Cavendish."

Brodie left the tavern.

In spite of the hour, he found a cabman who had dropped off a last fare of the night and paid him extra to take him to the Strand.

He'd returned to the office late, only to find that his key no longer worked, and Mr. Cavendish was not about, most likely with Miss Effie now that they were married.

The lock had been changed after a previous incident. And now?

He picked the lock and let himself in and reached for the button for the electric on the wall beside the entrance. At a glance, he took in the adjacent room, darkened and with no movement in reaction to the light that filled the office nor from the faint noise he'd made at the door.

Mikaela had no doubt returned to Mayfair for the night.

He preferred that she go there when he was making inquiries on his own, yet he felt the stillness and the quiet in the office in ways he hadn't noticed in a long time.

It was in the way she filled the office with her scratchings at the chalkboard, the sound of her pecking away at the machine on her desk as she made her notes, or in the sound of the cabinet door opening as she retrieved a bottle of Old Lodge and poured two glasses.

And in her observations about the particular inquiry case they were working. The way she had of standing before the chalkboard, studying what she'd written there. It was her curiosity, the way her mind worked, in ways he'd never known in a woman.

When had she become someone he needed, when he'd told himself that he didn't need anyone? Her spirit, her stubbornness, the courage that terrified him, and the way she understood the things in his past that few others even knew about?

He felt the nudge on his leg and looked down at the hound, unaware until that moment that he'd left the door to the office ajar.

"Aye, it's cold and ye smell like a garbage scow," he told him. "I've a notion to send ye back to the alcove."

He could have sworn the hound grinned at him.

He closed the door and went to the stove, as Rupert made a thorough inspection of the office, nose to the floor, then unexpectedly sat at a place beside Mikaela's desk.

"Ye can stay just until I get the fire built," he told the beast, as if he understood.

Brodie added pieces of coal and lit the fire. Then he went to the cabinet, retrieved the bottle of Old Lodge whisky, and poured a dram.

The hound refused to move.

Brodie was more than aware that Rupert had a special fondness for Mikaela that undoubtedly had to do with the food she provided him: sponge cake and biscuits.

He'd never had an animal of any kind as a pet or companion and considered the hound nothing more than a common street vagrant that smelled bad, especially when the weather set in and he'd been out and about on the street.

Still, there was an intelligence there, and the animal was protective of Mikaela and had been known to attack more than one who threatened her. Brodie was among those who seemed to have been accepted.

"He likes you, if you would give him a chance. He is quite intelligent and excellent at tracking a person down," she had reminded him.

"Wot is it?" he said to the hound as if he might answer.

Rupert whined then slowly made his way over to the fire. Brodie reached down and scratched him behind the ears as Mikaela had done hundreds of times.

"Aye, ye worthless vagrant, I miss her as well."

When the fire at the stove had taken the chill off the room and he had drained the last of the whisky from his glass, Brodie went into the adjacent bedroom.

He removed his jacket and boots, set the revolver on the table beside the bed, then dropped down onto the bed. Exhaustion, the cold from the streets, and the death of an old friend still waiting to be answered overcame him as the hound curled on the rug beside the bed.

Retired Detective Chief Inspector Jeremiah Dawes closed the wrought-iron gate and walked to the entrance of the modest terraced house in Hammersmith and inserted the key in the lock.

He immediately caught the scent of supper as he hung his coat and umbrella on the coat stand. Leg of lamb, if he wasn't mistaken, as he made his way to the sitting room.

"Good evening, Mrs. Marsh," he called out a greeting. "I'll be in the parlor."

There was no answer, not that he expected one, as he entered the parlor, then went to the coal stove.

It was cold in here, he thought with a frown. Mrs. Marsh should have set the fire hours ago with the weather that had set in.

It was just the two of them, except for the occasional visit by one of the men he once worked with. His wife had passed several years before, as had Mrs. Marsh's husband.

He had offered her a room, since she was there most days. It seemed a mutually beneficial solution when her rents were increased beyond what she could afford.

They got along. She managed the housekeeping and cooking, with Sundays off to visit her son. He kept to himself, meeting up with those he'd worked with, whose numbers were steadily growing fewer as the years passed.

Best get the fire lit, he thought.

He wadded paper from the day-old newspaper and placed it on the iron grate, then added pieces of coal from the bin beside the fireplace. He reached for the matches on the mantel.

"Eh?" he called out at a sound. "Is supper ready, Mrs. Marsh? It smells most delightful.

The blow caught him on the back of his shoulders and threw him against the mantel. He was dragged around, his attacker's fists clasped over the lapels of his coat. Stunned, he stared at the man who pinned him against the mantel.

"Who are you?!" he demanded. "What do you want?"

"Take a look," his attacker hissed.

The chief inspector fought to free himself as pale grey eyes glared back at him from sunken flesh.

"Take a long look and remember."

"Whoever you are... There is nothing of value here."

He was cut off once more.

"Nothing of value..." the man rasped. "That is what you made of me!"

The chief inspector shook his head.

"There must be some mistake. I don't know you..."

"You know me..." the words lashed at him. "You knew me then, nothing more than a report on paper, for you and the others!"

He was shaken then, no match for the man who had him pinned, or the insanity he saw in those pale eyes.

"Take a long look, Chief Inspector, and remember," his attacker hissed. "It will be your last."

"No! I don't know you..."

And then he did remember, back through the years, all the faces of all those who'd been arrested and brought before his desk.

"I see it now...you remember," his attacker snarled.

He saw it in the expression on the chief inspector's face. Then the disbelief as he brought the knife up and slashed it across his throat, and watched with grim satisfaction as blood soaked the front of Chief Inspector Dawe's shirt and that last thought slipped away on a gurgling gasp...

Six

BRODIE, #204 ON THE STRAND

THE SOUND WAS persistent and brought him up out of sleep and old dreams, followed by a snarling sound from the floor beside the bed. A glance at the window told him it was not yet morning as he reached for the revolver.

He went into the outer office, the hound beside him as the pounding on the door continued.

A stocky shadow showed through the door's glass panes in the pool of light from the landing. And then a voice—Inspector Dooley of the Metropolitan Police.

Brodie pocketed the revolver, turned on the electric in the office, then opened the door. The hound was there and made a thorough inspection of Mr. Dooley, then turned back to the warmth of the office.

"Wot has happened?" Brodie demanded.

Was it possible that the man who'd killed Constable Martin had been found? Yet, instinct told him different, along with the grim expression on Mr. Dooley's face.

"There's been another murder," Mr. Dooley replied as he shook the rain from his overcoat, then removed his hat and stepped into the office.

"The word came in from the district office, with a call made by the housekeeper," Dooley explained as he sat in the chair across the desk from Brodie.

"The poor woman was near hysterical after she found the Chief's Inspector's body."

He used the formal title even though the man had been retired for several years. The respect was there for a man they had both served under.

"She found him dead in the parlor, blood everywhere, as there seemed to have been quite a struggle."

"Did she see anyone?"

Mr. Dooley shook his head. "She went to let him know that supper was ready and found him. A neighbor nearby heard her screams and contacted the constable who patrols the area. Word was sent over to the station, and they put a call into me. The poor woman was near hysterical when I arrived."

"Has the residence been inspected?"

"Not as yet. I had a constable stationed there after the body was removed. Due to the chief inspector's long association with the MET, the people from CID will be called in. And then very likely the case will be handled by them."

Brodie nodded. The deaths of two persons connected to the MET within a handful of days. What did it mean? Was there something at the residence that might tell them something about who had done this?

"I know wot yer thinkin'," Mr. Dooley commented. "Ye want to see the place for yerself."

Brodie nodded. "Aye, before the Criminal Investigation

Department gets their hands into it. Ye know verra well how it works."

The C.I.D. had been established years before to take over the investigative side of crimes after a corruption scandal. They had the resources to investigate crimes, as he well knew. And with the murder of one of their own, they would be all over this. Then everything, all evidence, any possible leads, would be locked down, and the case very likely taken over by the New Scotland Yard.

Mr. Dooley agreed. "That will be the end of learnin' anything about what happened."

"I need to get inside the residence," Brodie replied. "Before they begin their investigation."

"The housekeeper is not about. She went to her sister's place last night. And I know well the man I placed on duty there. He's had his own encounter with the C.I.D., and he'll not say a word of your presence there if I ask it of him."

Brodie nodded. He needed to change clothes. The street clothes, as Mikaela called them, that he'd worn the day before, might well have the constable on duty call out the alarm at first sight.

His presence there would be far more acceptable if Dooley explained that he was there as a 'consultant' to the Metropolitan Police, a service he had provided from time to time in the past since he left the MET.

Abberline was another obstacle. It wouldn't be the first time, nor the last. For now, it was best to learn what he could before the man was involved. He was a political beast, and they'd had confrontations in the past that had seen the man put on suspension. There would be no cooperation from that quarter in this.

When he'd changed clothes and pocketed the revolver, he

left a hasty note for Mikaela, then followed Mr. Dooley out onto the landing along with the hound and set the lock in the door.

In spite of the early hour, Mr. Cavendish had arrived. The flat he now shared with Miss Effie was behind the Public House and very near the office.

"There's a problem with the lock on the office door, I had to pick the lock last night," Brodie told him, a reminder to get the lock repaired.

"It's locked now."

"It had to be changed," Mr. Cavendish informed him as he reached inside his jacket pocket, retrieved a new key, and handed it to him.

"Miss Mikaela found the office door open when she arrived yesterday."

That stopped him. "Open? It was secure when I was last here, and she would not have been so careless to leave it unlocked. Was anythin' taken?"

"She said there didn't appear to be anything missing. Then, had me contact the locksmith."

Brodie nodded as he pocketed the new key.

He was certain neither of them left the office unlocked. That could only mean that someone had picked the lock, then continued inside.

But for wot reason? And nothin' missing? With her typing machine and the few personal items they kept there, there was almost nothing of value.

Or was the door tampered with for some reason other than thievery?

Did that explain the hound's peculiar behavior the night before, the animal's thorough inspection of the place, and then his reaction near her desk?

Mikaela's scent would be there, of course. Yet, had the hound sensed someone else?

"Aye, ye did well, Mr. Cavendish. I've left a note for her when she returns." He glanced down at the hound on the sidewalk.

It was instinct and might mean nothing at all. Still, with himself off and about and her as well, and the realization that someone had been inside the office?

"You might have Miss Effie provide food for the hound, and tell Miss Mikaela when ye see her that she should keep him with her."

Mr. Cavendish grinned. "I will do that. And be careful yerself, sir."

Brodie nodded.

Mr. Dooley had used one of the public transit drivers instead of a constable provided by the MET and held the driver over when he arrived.

They climbed into the coach and Mr. Dooley provided the late chief inspector's address in Hammersmith.

The constable who had been positioned outside the entrance of the terrace home was young, perhaps new to the force, Brodie thought as they arrived. Mr. Dooley gave him a cursory nod.

"A consultant with the MET," he told the young constable by way of introduction, and they entered the residence.

There was no one inside as the housekeeper had taken herself off to her sister's house in another part of the city.

Supper had obviously been prepared, a single place set at the small dining table with a covered pot of food, the scent still in the air.

Mr. Dooley turned on the electric, and they went into the

small parlor where the chief inspector's body had been found by the poor woman.

There were obvious things that stood out when inspecting the scene of a crime—signs of a struggle, things overturned, drawers emptied in the situation of a robbery, blood from the victim if the attacker had been caught in the act.

Yet here, nothing was disturbed. There was no indication that the attack had been for the purpose of robbery. Still, there were signs of a struggle in front of the hearth.

"The body was found just there on the floor," Mr. Dooley explained. "It seems that the chief inspector was caught unawares from behind. As you see, there was a struggle before the person took the knife to him."

"Did the housekeeper mention anything of value that might have been taken?"

"She was upset, as you can well imagine. But she did say that it didn't seem that anything was taken."

Apparently not robbery, Brodie thought. Although the attacker might have been caught and then fled.

"Did the body have anything of value on it?" Brodie asked. "He always carried a pocket watch."

"I'll make the inquiry regarding that with the morgue where the body was taken," Mr. Dooley responded.

Brodie went to the hearth. There were obvious signs of a struggle in scuff marks in the ash on the wood floor in front of the hearth where the chief inspector had fought with his attacker, along with a good amount of dried blood.

A mark caught his attention, and he took out his hand-held lamp and turned it on, then knelt to inspect it closer as he aimed the beam at the floor. It appeared to be a boot mark.

"Ye saw the body?" he asked Mr. Dooley.

"I arrived shortly after the wagon was sent for by the constable who was first to see it after the housekeeper found him."

"Wot was the chief inspector wearing?"

"Trousers, shirt with vest and jacket over, as he had just arrived after being out earlier."

"I need to see the body and the clothes he was wearin'," Brodie replied.

What he had found might mean nothing at all, or it could be important.

"With the New Scotland Yard to be in charge of the situation, that could be difficult," Dooley pointed out.

Brodie nodded. "There is someone who may be able to assist."

Someone he had previously made the acquaintance of in the course of an inquiry case. He might be willing to assist, as it was in the matter of the murder of a chief inspector of police.

For this he needed to send a formal request to meet with the man, something that Mikaela most usually would have taken care of in the past.

But she had her own inquiry case, and truth was that he didn't want her involved in this.

MIKAELA

Brodie hadn't returned to Mayfair the night before, not that it was unexpected, particularly when he was off making inquiries among people he knew from his past work with the Metropolitan Police.

I was very aware of that other part of his life and accepted that it was necessary from time to time. It was, after all, the nature of the inquiry business.

While I might have argued the matter, and had in the past, insisting that I was perfectly capable of taking care of myself in most situations, I respected his professional experience in such matters. Still...

"These are not the sort of places that would be safe for a woman," he had told me more than once, and then with that familiar half-smile at one corner of his mouth.

"They are places I'm familiar with, and the people I know. And I wouldn't put it past someone to do ye harm out of spite. After all, ye are an attractive woman and a person of means. It is best I make my inquiries while ye complete pursuit of the case to Lady Ambersley. And dinna fash."

Don't worry. Yes, well, that was easier said than done, and I had patched up more than one of his wounds in the past.

Bloody, stubborn Scot!

It was one of those things that I struggled with, when I had told myself for most of my life that I didn't need anyone. Other than my sister and my great-aunt.

'The best laid schemes of mice and men often go awry.'

So said another Scot.

'So, here you are,' that irritating little voice inside me whispered. *'What are you to do?'*

Get on with it! I thought.

There was Kitty Ambersley and her very valuable, still missing necklace. I did have a thought about that, and I was determined to meet with her as soon as possible.

After my third cup of coffee and notes made in my notebook, I placed a telephone call to the Ambersley residence.

I pushed back the somewhat sarcastic thought, not for the first time—who in the world went by the name of 'Kitty'?

The next thought that followed—who would have a dog named Bitsy carried around in a handbag?

To each their own, I thought.

After all, I preferred the company of a somewhat disreputable hound that liked sponge cake and had a habit of dragging up dead creatures dropped at my feet like a trophy.

It was with that thought in mind that I called for a cab, then dressed for my meeting with Lady Kitty Ambersley.

When Mrs. Ryan announced that the driver had arrived, I took a piece of ham I had not eaten from my breakfast plate, wrapped it in my napkin, and tucked it into my travel bag.

As I did so, my fingers brushed the revolver Brodie insisted that I carry when I was off and about on my own.

There was a fleeting thought that involved Bitsy. I pushed it back.

Upon my arrival at the Ambersley residence, I was greeted by the head butler, who assured me that Lady Ambersley would join me presently.

Tea was provided as I overheard a distant yapping sound that I recognized as Bitsy, who arrived along with Kitty Ambersley and promptly darted past in my direction.

There was a moment where that sharp little gaze met mine, and Bitsy slid to a stop, rude creature that he was.

Not that I think the little bit of fluff was intelligent enough to understand the folly in attacking me once more, although I am convinced that the hound understands a great deal. Anything was possible.

It was a wise move on Bitsy's part that he then returned to the edge of the carpet and promptly lifted a leg on a Queen

Anne chair, which necessitated the summons of a footman to remedy the situation.

My earlier thought returned. I ignored it. This was Kitty Ambersley's home. She could do with it as she wished.

"Do forgive the situation. He does that when he's excited."

Of course.

Over the course of the next hour, I explained my conversations with both ladies who were present at the Ambersley's supper party.

"Oh, dear. I had so hoped that one of them might have seen something," Kitty Ambersley commented, with Bitsy at her feet glaring at me.

"What is to be done now?" she inquired.

"I did have a thought in the matter," I replied. "With your permission?"

"Of course, if it will be useful," she agreed.

I removed the napkin with the piece of ham wrapped within and dropped it to the carpet. Quick as a wink, Bitsy darted across the space between where we sat, snatched up the napkin, then shot out of the drawing room and down the hallway.

"Oh my," Kitty Ambersley exclaimed. "Whatever has gotten into him?"

Indeed, I thought, as I quickly followed, and encountered a footman who indicated the direction the little thief had gone.

To say the situation caused quite an uproar is a bit of an understatement. Bitsy was a fast little devil, but I was not about to be outrun.

I ran as I followed his path into the main hall, up the stairs to the second-floor chambers, past a startled maid, who indicated the bed chamber at the end of the hall, and discovered that Bitsy seemed to have disappeared.

This would have been far simpler if I'd brought Rupert with me. However, I couldn't guarantee the safety of Bitsy if the hound was set upon him.

This was obviously the lady's bedchamber with an adjoining bathing chamber, a vast closet full of fine clothing. I heard the faint sound of growling as I approached the bed.

The entire household seemed to have joined in the chase as I heard voices from the hallway beyond, including that of Lady Ambersley as I knelt beside the bed, then threw back the satin coverlet.

I was immediately greeted by a snarling sound as I discovered Bitsy in the looming darkness under the bed with the piece of ham wrapped in a napkin clutched in its teeth amid other 'treasures.'

Those treasures included a pair of men's underdrawers, no doubt belonging to Lord Ambersley—they were made of silk, which would not be worn by a servant. There was also a dead bird that had obviously been there for some time as it was quite shrunken, and something wrapped in a dinner napkin.

I retrieved the object rolled in the other napkin. Let Bitsy enjoy the ham, I thought, the servants could attend to the dead bird and underdrawers, as I retreated from under the bed and stood triumphantly with the other napkin in hand.

It was quite heavy, just as Lady Ambersley had told me when recounting that evening when the necklace had dropped into her soup. She had then retrieved it and wrapped it in her napkin, no doubt thinking to have it cleaned after the supper party.

However, covered in a hearty soup then set aside, it had provided a tempting target for a skilled thief with four legs. As I unwrapped the napkin, the jewels gleaming through haze of dried soup, I suspected there were undoubtedly other 'treasures' hidden under the bed and perhaps in other places as well.

"My necklace!" Lady Ambersley exclaimed as she hurried across the room. "However did you think to look there?" she inquired.

I didn't bother to explain that it was experience with another sort of 'thief' or that she was fortunate that it was the necklace and not some dead creature left rotting under her bed.

I would have to reward Rupert for the idea. Perhaps a biscuit with jam. He was quite fond of them.

"I am so very grateful," Kitty Ambersley thanked me once again. "I will speak to the servants. It seems they have been somewhat remiss in their cleaning efforts."

Of course, I thought, with another suggestion—banning Bitsy to the gardens where he could relieve himself without repercussions. And possibly an encounter with a hawk or other scavenger?

Admittedly, it was dreadful to contemplate, yet the creature was quite deserving.

It was early in the afternoon as I prepared to leave. There had been the usual conversation about the value of the necklace that she would promptly take to her jeweler to be cleaned. I reminded her of the clasp.

Then there was the additional conversation over small finger sandwiches she had served for luncheon. Bitsy was such a rascal, but such a sweet creature, she insisted, extolling his virtues while I glared at him and silently dared him to come near.

And then there was the matter of our fee.

"Of course. I shall have my banker send payment for your services by courier," she assured me. "I do so appreciate that you found my necklace."

And I *appreciated* that I would not be forced to share further company with Bitsy.

Lady Ambersley insisted on providing her driver to take me wherever I needed to go.

I did appreciate the gesture and directed him to the office on the Strand where I hoped there might be some word from Brodie.

Seven

MIKAELA

MR. CAVENDISH WAS NOT ABOUT, and the office on the second story landing was darkened.

It seemed that Brodie had returned at some point, the bedcovers rumpled as if he had been restless. Then I discovered the note he had left for me.

I smiled. It was very much in the style of a police report, much the same as he had no doubt written countless times when he was with the MET.

It was straight forward, an update on his own efforts in the matter of Constable Martin's death, then a brief inquiry about the Ambersley case.

I may be some time in this matter. I hope this finds you well. B.

So much for endearments.

Never let it be said that Brodie was effusive about his feelings, not even so much as a brief comment that he missed me.

81

Yet, as I knew only too well, there was always something behind those very business-like comments and lack of endearments if one looked closely. And I did.

"Ye are the one with the skill at words, with yer novels and the reports ye write up on your type writing machine," he had told me more than once. "Ye are far better at it than m'self."

I suspected it was simply his way of avoiding lengthy reports. Better at it, indeed.

What did you expect? That little voice inside my head whispered. *It's the way of the man. You have certainly known others who were long on words and lacking in all other ways.*

Most certainly, I thought, as I straightened the office, then went to the chalkboard and made my final notes regarding the resolution of the Ambersley case.

I then decided to spend the next couple of hours on my next Emma novel.

I had created a character who was most fond of adventures and had taken herself off on several of them, until her path had crossed that of a mysterious dark haired, dark-eyed man who provided private inquiry services in a series of very dangerous cases.

There had been eight Emma Fortescue novels to date, regarded by the newspapers as somewhat less than literary classics in their pithy comments when the books were mentioned at all. Yet Emma's adventures were adored by a readership across London that included not only women but men as well.

There had been a somewhat fascinating conversation with Brodie when he learned there was an obvious resemblance to our work, not to mention our relationship.

"Ye canna write about anyone in the royal family," he had reminded me at the time. "Or ye might find yerself bundled off to Newgate prison for revealing important information."

Of course, dear.

I understood perfectly well, and in conversation with my publisher over the matter, had simply changed the names and a few of the details in the '*adventures*' that Emma Fortescue found herself in. Not to mention her working partnership with a particular individual who happened to be a Scot.

The books were reviewed, including a warning that they might not be appropriate for proper ladies and young women to read. The critic's objection: The somewhat colorful details of inquiry cases and a growing relationship between Emme Fortescue and the mysterious man she had thrown in with to solve the murder of a man she had once known.

Scandal books, they were called by those who wrote for the dailies, specifically Theodolphus Burke, writer for the Times. And in spite of the not-subtle warning that they were not suitable for respectable ladies and young women, the sales of that first book, and the other ones that followed, had been quite incredible.

My publisher and also my brother-in-law, was ecstatic with the success of the Emma Books as he called them.

It did seem as if the women and ladies of London and beyond were not of the same opinion as the newspaper writers and critics. And more recently, there was an inquiry from a New York publisher to publish them there.

I inserted a piece of paper into the typing machine, then turned and studied my notes for the Ambersley case on the chalkboard.

The names would have to be changed, of course, along with a few of the details. With a flash of inspiration, I typed the first paragraph of my new book:

'*The little dog fit nicely into Lady Montcrief's handbag, nipping at anyone who came near.*

The hound, stalwart veteran of countless encounters with wild beasts and fowl, regarded the creature like its next meal.

Emma Fortescue would need to keep a watchful eye on the hound.

He did have a habit of doing-in bothersome pests. Not precisely murder, yet offensive to some persons, particularly those with small, irritating pets that resembled hairy rats.'

It would need some editing, I thought. Those who carried their pets around in handbags would undoubtedly take offense.

Still, my publisher had received several letters hailing the previous adventures of the stalwart hound who had participated in our inquiry cases.

"It does seem as if you have acquired an audience," I mentioned to said hound, who lay on the floor beside my desk.

I admit that the look he gave me then bore a resemblance to another look I often received from Brodie when extolling the hound's virtues.

'Scepticism' was not quite right. It was more a look as if I had taken complete leave of my senses.

"Next, ye'll be tellin' me that he understands everythin' ye say."

I simply smiled at that

It was very near midday when the hound rose from the floor beside my desk, stretched, then went to the office door. An obvious sign that his morning nap was concluded.

I followed him down the stairs with the thought that Brodie might have returned, only to discover that Mr. Cavendish had arrived quite late—unusual for him, or possibly delayed by some errand.

"Good day, miss," he greeted me as the hound charged

across the thoroughfare with particular enthusiasm that could only mean food was involved.

I glanced across the Strand. Rupert had a working arrangement with the man who sold sandwiches from his cart. In exchange for food, the hound stood guard against anyone making off without paying for their sandwich.

He was an enterprising sort.

I inquired about Miss Effie, as she and Mr. Cavendish had recently married, something that always brought a smile to his face. However, the smile was not there at present.

"Well enough, and workin' her shift at the public house," he replied, somewhat distracted, which made me think there might be some difficulty there.

A newsboy appeared with the usual enthusiasm for a sale, the last issues of the morning edition of the Times tucked under his arm.

He could have been no more than nine or ten, with dark hair that fell across his forehead and dark eyes that reminded me of someone else.

"Paper for you, miss?" he inquired.

"Be off with you," Mr. Cavendish told him.

I had not read the morning paper that included the crime sheet before leaving Mayfair and thought there might be an update from the MET in the matter of Constable Martin's death.

I took a coin from the pocket of my skirt.

The newsboy's smile was restored as he took the coin and handed me the morning paper, then ran off after another sale.

"I noticed that Mr. Brodie returned the evening past," I commented to Mr. Cavendish after he left.

He nodded, not quite meeting my gaze, an obvious indication that he knew more than he was sharing.

"Did he say where he was off to next in the matter of the case he's pursuing?"

"Mr. Brodie keeps things to himself as you well know, miss."

Hmmm, yes, I thought. Definitely something there that he was not telling me. Perhaps on Brodie's instructions?

Brodie had been particularly reserved since Constable Martin's death and insisted that I continue with the Ambersley case, which was now resolved, while he made his usual inquiries.

I was aware that Constable Martin had been a good friend as well as partner when Brodie first joined the MET, and then afterward when he became an inspector.

Though he rarely mentioned his time with the Metropolitan, he had spoken often of Constable Martin, usually when in the company of Mr. Dooley or Mr. Conner, who had both worked with him as well.

"You will let me know if you hear from him," I reminded Mr. Cavendish.

He nodded, "That I will, miss." Still without meeting my gaze.

I turned toward the lift by the alcove, then paused as I heard my name through the noise of coaches, carts, and wagons at the Strand.

"Lady Forsythe? I've a message from the Home Office."

It was George Endicott, one of several dispatchers from the messenger service Brodie and I frequently used.

He was young, fair, with a warm brown gaze that bordered on flirtation, and a most engaging smile.

"That would be for me," Mr. Cavendish attempted to intercept Mr. Endicott.

George looked at me somewhat confused.

"Lady Forsythe?"

"I'll take it, if you please."

He handed me the envelope, then the clipboard he carried.

I did notice that the envelope had my name on it as well as Brodie's.

"If you'll sign here. I was told to deliver it straightaway."

There was that engaging smile again.

When I offered him the usual coin for the delivery, he shook his head.

"It was already taken care of by Mr. Cavendish when he sent the message earlier. Good day."

Most interesting. That did explain his absence earlier from his usual place at the alcove.

I looked down at the envelope after George left.

"From the Home Office?"

Mr. Cavendish seemed uncomfortable.

"Beg your pardon, miss. He said there was no need for you to know, what with the other case you were working on."

"I understand. He had you deliver the message to the courier service. And how were you to reach him when this arrived?"

"He said that he'd be round for it."

I tucked the newspaper under my arm. With the envelope in hand, I returned to the office.

The envelope from the Home Office was apparently in response to something Brodie had requested regarding his inquiry into the death of Constable Martin.

It was addressed to both of us, no doubt owing to our previous inquiry cases with assistance from the office of the Home Secretary, and my acquaintance with Mr. Asquith through my great-aunt.

I had laid the envelope on Brodie's desk, then went to my own desk with the morning paper.

I scanned the front page, which contained a fair amount of gossip, along with an interesting article regarding a certain disquieting event in Paris during a political conference that had been disturbed by an explosion that had come dangerously close to injuring several attendees.

The names that appeared were representatives of heads of state from several countries across Europe.

It did seem as if the situation on the Continent might be simmering with an undercurrent of unrest.

I had travelled through most of the large cities in Europe on my adventures and had seen some of the discontent in groups that gathered at the rail stations and at government buildings.

I understood the reasons for discontent, yet the deaths of innocent people caught up in the violence were enormously sad and highly disturbing.

The rest of the news of the day was the usual sort—the 'personals' page with notices submitted for those seeking companionship, marriage, and one soliciting for a person to share accommodation. I could only imagine what that might mean. I then turned to the crime sheet.

Brodie was convinced that I had a peculiar fascination for crime, yet there was the possibility that there might be information regarding the case he was investigating, considering that the death of Constable Martin was about one of their own.

I sat up as I noticed an additional paragraph on the attack and death in the late hours of the day before, of Mr. J. Dawes in Hammersmith, retired Chief Inspector with the Metropolitan Police. It ended with a statement that an investigation by the MET was presently in progress.

That name was familiar. Brodie had mentioned it only days before when he received word from Mr. Dooley about the death of Constable Martin. Jerome Dawes had been Chief Inspector of Police where both Brodie and Constable Martin had been assigned when Brodie served with the MET!

Was Brodie aware of what had now happened? I glanced at the envelope that had been delivered by courier.

Mr. Asquith, the Home Secretary, had been most accommodating in the past in difficult situations.

The hound made a sound that might have been disapproval...if one believed that animals were capable of such things.

"What are you looking at?"

The hound simply rolled his eyes.

The envelope had been addressed to me as well. It was possible that I might be able to assist in some manner. I went to his desk, seized the envelope, and opened it.

In response to your request, the Home Secretary has contacted the necessary parties at New Scotland Yard and advised you are to be
provided every accommodation in the matter of the death of Chief
Inspector Dawes, late of the Metropolitan Police.
You are to keep the Home Secretary advised of your progress.

It was signed by Sidney Fairfield, Undersecretary to Mr. Asquith, the Home Secretary.

So, Brodie was aware of the death of the chief inspector. That, along with the fact that he had chosen to contact the Home Secretary, made it quite obvious that he was pursuing information in Dawes's death as well.

Two murders. Constable Martin and now the retired chief inspector, whom both men had served under.

Were they somehow connected?

Brodie had been quite clear that my assistance was not needed since I had my own inquiries to make on behalf of Kitty Ambersley.

Yet, the case I had had been resolved.

Two persons could make inquiries far more efficiently than one, as I had pointed out in the past. Even Mr. Holmes worked in partnership with an associate.

I returned the note to the envelope, gathered my notebook and tucked it into my bag, then called for Rupert.

I handed the envelope to Mr. Cavendish when I arrived at the sidewalk on the street below the office.

"Please see that Mr. Brodie receives this as soon as he returns. It is important."

It was very possible that the C.I.D., the criminal investigation division at New Scotland Yard, had information that might be useful.

In the meantime, there was someone I wanted to question in the matter. That paragon of virtue and truth, Theodolphus Burke of the Times.

He was admittedly one of the most detestable persons I had ever encountered: sneaky, conniving, and, to quote something Brodie once said of the man, *'he would no doubt sell his mother for a lead on a story.'*

I had the dubious privilege of experiencing each of those attributes, aside from selling his mother, and had managed to navigate my way around his schemes by making him an offer that someone of his low morals could not possibly refuse.

His weakness—that insatiable appetite for the 'story' that would provide him the enviable advantage of being able to be the first to report about one of London's more sensational crimes of the moment.

It was a bargain impossible for him to refuse, considering his low character. It was merely a matter of staying a few steps ahead of him.

Brodie had initially disapproved of using the man's unscrupulous methods for getting the story before his fellow reporters at the other tabloids. However, he was forced to admit that an exchange of information in the past had provided valuable clues in solving a case.

I hailed a cab and gave the driver the address of the Times newspaper offices, then climbed into the cab. Rupert immediately followed.

I didn't argue the matter. Like another, he could be quite stubborn.

"If you must," I commented. He looked up at me from the floor of the cab and grinned.

Eight

BRODIE, #204 THE STRAND

THE DRIVER of the coal cart let him off at the edge of
Piccadilly—it was beyond his usual route, and he would go no
farther. The man wanted to get on with his deliveries.

Brodie walked the rest of the way, cutting down cross-
streets, past the usual street vendors and the Public House,
even though he hadn't eaten since the day before.

There had been no time after he met with Mr. Dooley at
Chief Inspector Dawes's residence.

There was exhaustion along with hunger from not having
eaten since the day before, but he was used to that from
another life...

Street vendors were not precisely in abundance in the
places he had been. But it was not the hunger that drove him
down an alley, across another street, until he emerged at the
Strand, then made his way toward the office.

If Mr. Cavendish had followed his instructions, there

might be a response from the message he'd had him send. And that was what he looked for now.

Head down, his collar turned up against the rain and cold, he dodged the usual foot traffic on the sidewalk until the roofline of the office came into view. He crossed the thoroughfare with an eye to the traffic, then walked the short distance to the office building.

Mr. Cavendish gave him a nod as he reached the sidewalk at the bottom of the stairs that led up to the office.

The windows on the second floor were dark, which told him that Mikaela was not there. That would have brought questions about the progress he'd made. Not to mention the message he hoped to find in answer to the request he'd had Mr. Cavendish send round to the Home Office.

He could have sworn the man ducked his head as he reached inside his coat, pulled out an envelope, and handed it to him.

"The response you were waitin' for."

Brodie took the envelope, noticed the embossed address of the Home Office, and retrieved the note inside.

"When did this arrive?" he asked Mr. Cavendish.

There was an uneasy glance again.

"A bit more than an hour ago."

Brodie nodded. "And Lady Forsythe?"

"She was here earlier and worked up at the office for a time. It seems she finished with the inquiries she was making."

If Mr. Cavendish had legs, Brodie was certain he would have shuffled his feet. The man was definitely put off by something.

He turned the envelope over and noticed the two names at the front.

"Was she here when this arrived?"

Another hesitant nod. "She took it from the courier, went up to the office, then took herself off with the hound."

After she had undoubtedly read it.

"Aye," Brodie replied as he tucked the note into his coat pocket, then climbed the stairs to the office.

MIKAELA

Upon arriving at the Times offices, I looked down at Rupert at the sidewalk. He sat, waiting expectantly.

He could be most congenial, particularly where food was involved. However, there were other instances where he had shown a rather aggressive nature. Particularly where Theodolphus Burke was concerned. He did seem to have a dislike of the man.

"Behave yourself," I told him as we entered the lobby of the building.

"Good day," the young man at the desk greeted me with a faintly bemused glance down at the hound.

We had met previously, and I had discovered that he was not only an aspiring writer for the newspaper who had been relegated to the front desk for 'experience,' as he mentioned at the time, but we shared a similar opinion of Mr. Burke. He also had a particular liking for the hound.

"Mr. Burke is in his office this afternoon. Should I announce your arrival, or is it to be a surprise?" he commented somewhat cheekily, as Burke had a tendency to leave the building by another means if the situation was not to his liking.

"No need," I replied. "We do know our way."

"Have a pleasant visit," he responded with amusement.

With that, I proceeded to the lift with Rupert.

As we had both been to the newsroom previously, there was only a brief nod of acknowledgement when we arrived at the floor where the staff reporters had their desks lined up in an open space.

Two reporters pecked away at typing machines while others wrote information down in notebooks. One, a young staff writer by the name of Edward Ealing, greeted me from the counter as an older gentleman grabbed his coat from a coat rack in quite a rush, cap askew on his head, notebook in hand.

"Where are you off to, Mr. Casey?" he inquired.

"I'm meeting with Mr. Holmes," he replied somewhat crankily. "He's finally agreed to discuss his latest case."

I nodded as he passed by with a tip of his cap. I did wish him luck with that. It was widely known that Mr. Holmes could be somewhat erratic in his habits, particularly where newspaper people were concerned.

I had met Mr. Holmes once at a reception upon the release of one of my Emma books.

He had entered the shop unrecognizable in a disguise and merely wandered about until most of the people had left. He then approached the table as I was preparing to leave as well.

I do not claim that he actually complimented me on the thinly disguised plot of my book that closely mirrored the first case Brodie and I had pursued. Instead, he stood back, watching me with just one word. "*Fascinating.*"

There followed a brief discussion about what that might mean.

"*It is fascinating that a woman would write such a grisly tale,*" he had explained. "*But then, I suppose one may write anything they might imagine. It is, after all, fiction.*"

Yes, well. I wouldn't go so far as to say he was condescending. However, I was tempted to explain the specific case I had written about more thoroughly. Although fictionalized to protect certain persons.

Instead, I simply replied, "The bullet wound has healed quite nicely, although there is a rather nasty scar."

Mr. Holmes burst out laughing. *"You remind me of someone I know—beautiful, charming, and a bit dangerous."*

We had discussed several points in my book, which he eventually conceded was a 'rather nice little tome.'

And then, a thought in parting. *"Do keep up the good work, Lady Forsythe. There are far too many evil persons in the world. And poor writers."*

It was a most unusual encounter. However, I considered it a compliment that Mr. Holmes had taken the time to engage in conversation.

I noticed in a quick glance that Mr. Burke was not among those in the newsroom.

He had been provided a private office once more after a fall from grace, as it were. I turned at the hallway that led to that office.

His door was closed. I knocked lightly, did not wait for a response as he would surely have told me to go away, then opened the door and stepped inside.

"I left instructions that I was not to be disturbed if I am to meet this deadline," he announced without looking up.

"Then I shall only take a few minutes of your time," I replied.

His head came up. "I would say that it is a pleasure, Lady Forsythe. However..."

He abruptly pushed back from the desk and seized his umbrella as if it was a weapon.

"And what the devil is that animal doing here!?"

"As you well know, he is quite docile unless provoked," I replied. "And he has a particular dislike of umbrellas."

He slowly lowered the weaponized umbrella. Rupert immediately sat down but kept a watchful eye on him.

"I have a deadline to meet..." Burke snapped as he returned to his chair.

"As I explained, I shall only take a few minutes of your time. It is in the matter of an article you wrote for the morning edition of the Times. The one about the murder of Chief Inspector Dawes as well as the murder of Constable Joseph Martin while he was on patrol in Piccadilly two nights previous."

I knew from past experience that Mr. Burke often knew a great deal more about a story than he initially revealed. He had been known to gradually reveal information in subsequent, often sensational, articles to keep readers purchasing additional editions of the newspaper to read his crime reporting.

He slowly looked up. "What do you want? Tell me, so that you will then leave."

I retrieved the morning edition from my bag and laid it on his desk.

"A most interesting article about the murder of Constable Martin and now the suspicious death of the retired Chief Inspector," I commented.

"Considering your talent as a reporter," I continued, "you undoubtedly have additional information that you have learned regarding the two situations."

"Situations?" he repeated. "You always put everything so very proper that no one could possibly detect the threat behind it."

"I have no idea what you are speaking of," I replied.

"The fact that your great-aunt is Lady Antonia Montgomery and an acquaintance of long-standing and some influ-ence with Mr. Walter, who is now owner of the Times."

There was that, of course. Something I had learned after my first inquiry case. Her opinion of Theodolphus Burke was much the same as my own.

"Pompous, arrogant little man with hardly a teaspoon of talent," she had commented in that particular conversation. "All he is capable of writing about are sensational crimes like those poor women murdered in the East End. And those have yet to be solved."

Aunt Antonia was an avid patron of the Times. Still there was Burke's point about her acquaintance with Mr. Walter.

"There is little known at this time about the murders," he informed me. "You, above all, should know that you cannot divulge everything you know."

His tone brought a low growl from Rupert.

"I do not know which is the more threatening, Lady Forsythe. That scroungy beast or yourself."

I took that as a compliment. However, I wasn't so certain about Rupert. His hackles were still raised on his back.

"How is it that you learned so quickly about what had happened to the chief inspector?"

"I have my sources, just as you and Mr. Brodie."

I gave him a long look. "Someone within the MET no doubt."

"When the call came in from the constable on duty nearby, a 'friend' contacted me. I will not share his name, even under risk of peril."

This was said with a look in Rupert's direction. It was too tempting.

"Was there a particular reason you were contacted?" I replied.

He made a sound, very much like a groan.

"I had met recently with the chief inspector about a project he was pursuing and had met with him at the old Scotland Yard, months past."

"Might I ask, what sort of project?"

"You might ask."

I waited.

"He wanted information about an old case that I had written about. He asked to see the newspaper archive about the case, and we had struck up an acquaintance."

I couldn't imagine that, yet to each their own.

"What was the case?"

"It was a case that I covered regarding one of your own, Sir Edward Blackwood, who was convicted of murdering a fellow gentleman, Sir Andrew Sark, in a duel. It caused quite a sensation at the time."

I could imagine, since dueling had been outlawed years before.

I knew of it in that way that gossip made its way around, even across the channel. But I didn't know the details of it, as I had been at school in Paris at the time. I did remember Aunt Antonia writing about it in one of her letters.

"I asked him if he was writing a book," Burke continued. "He denied it with an excuse that it was for other reasons."

"Were you able to provide the information he wanted?" I inquired.

"The archive at the Gazette was somewhat lacking, there was only the mention of it and the trial that followed. The writers at the Gazette were not of a high quality. It was the reason I left just prior for the Times."

Of course, I thought.

"When did you last meet with your source?" I then inquired.

"Tuesday, the week past."

"Did he share anything with you about being threatened by anyone?"

"That is all I will tell you, Lady Forsythe. Out of respect for the poor man."

I retrieved the newspaper and tucked it into my bag.

It would be helpful to make my own inquiries when it came to the Times archive. I was already aware that Burke would not share information.

"Will you now please leave?" he asked. "I have a deadline."

Undoubtedly for one of the lurid, sensational stories that he was known for.

"You have been most helpful,"

"And take the filthy animal with you!" he called after.

The 'filthy animal' that was somewhat cleaner than usual waited until I left the office, then bounded after me.

It was afternoon when I returned to the office, the usual wintry darkness settling in over the Strand with streetlights gleaming through the gloom of the fog that had set in, the bloody *haar*, as a Scot I knew quite well called it. Lights shone in the second story windows of the office as well.

The hound leapt down as the cab rolled to a stop.

"When did Mr. Brodie return?" I inquired as I stepped down.

"A short while ago," Mr. Cavendish informed me. "I gave him the envelope. He's been up there since, but said he would need a driver before end of day."

It seemed that he intended to visit the Yard yet that afternoon. I gathered my skirt in hand and ran up the stairs.

There were times when the stairs were far more expedient and held less danger than the lift stalling between the ground and second floors, although I wouldn't have admitted that to Brodie.

He preferred the stairs and insisted upon using them, even in nasty weather, stating more than once that he had no use for a box that might trap him. I had pointed out that there was a roof hatch for such situations.

"Which would not be necessary if lifts worked the way they're supposed to," he had grumbled in response.

He could be quite stubborn.

He was in the room adjacent to the outer office that served as a private bedroom when we stayed over.

I heard the distinct sound of the wardrobe door being closed rather sharply, then Brodie emerged wearing dress wool trousers, a white shirt that he tucked into the waist of the trousers, and a vest, obviously thrown on somewhat hastily as his shirt gaped open, unbuttoned.

A stirring sight to be certain.

He looked up, a frown showing through the obvious fatigue of the past few days, from wherever his inquiries regarding Constable Martin's murder had taken him.

He fumbled with his tie, a frequent battle that he usually conceded. I laid my travel bag on my desk and crossed the office to where he struggled.

I brushed his hands aside and noticed that the lines at the corners of his eyes and about his mouth slowly eased as I tied the strands of silk.

"I knew there was some reason that I keep ye about," he commented, the smell of soap mingling with that of pipe tobacco, and possibly some other fragrance that was vaguely familiar.

Such endearing sentiments.

"Mr. Cavendish mentioned that ye finished yer inquiries regarding Lady Ambersley's missing necklace."

"With some assistance from Aunt Antonia and Bitsy."

"And that would be?"

"My aunt is acquainted with Lady Ambersley. It seems that she has a habit of losing her necklace. She recalled a similar incident. And then there is Bitsy."

Dark brows arched. "I'm almost afraid to ask. Is it anythin' like Miss Templeton's lizard?"

He was referring to Ziggy, my good friend's iguana, a gift from a 'friend' on one of her tours.

"Bitsy is a purse pet, a very small dog. Lady Ambersley takes her everywhere.

"It seems that Bitsy has made off with things in the past and hidden them about the manor. The night the necklace disappeared, Lord and Lady Ambersley hosted a supper party." I then explained how the necklace became displaced in Kitty Ambersley's soup, that retrieved and wrapped in a linen napkin, then set aside.

"It seems that Bitsy made off with it when no one was aware and added it to her collection of treasures under Lord and Lady Ambersley's bed. A horde that included a pair of his silk underdrawers, a dead bird from the gardens, and the necklace."

Those dark eyes narrowed.

"Lord Ambersley's underdrawers?"

"Silk and quite large," I explained as I finished tying his tie and laid my hands against the front of his shirt. I blocked out the image of Lord Ambersley and his overlarge drawers.

"I am most appreciative of yourself," I complimented him.

"Is that so?"

"Yes, and now I may be of assistance with your inquiries," I added.

"I appreciate that," he told me. "I truly do, but I've already had to go into places and speak with a good many disreputable persons I would not want ye to be around."

"Someone who wears rather cheap cologne?" I commented regarding that 'other' fragrance that lingered about him.

It was something I had encountered a few years earlier on a particular lady in a chartreuse gown who had been escaping his office rather early on the morning when I first sought his investigative services in the matter of the disappearance of my sister.

"Wot are ye blatherin' about, woman?"

"I made the acquaintance of the woman when I first inquired about your services," I suggested.

I caught the confusion in his expression, which I suspected was probably genuine. He shook his head and laughed.

"Are ye jealous, lass?"

"As someone we both know once told me…" And to quote the particular 'someone' standing before me, "I do not share what is mine."

"That would be Maudie," he replied. "She is an old friend, and she knew Constable Martin as well. He relied on her for information from time to time. I thought she might know something that could be useful."

"So you say," I teased.

He pulled me against him. "And where might yer travels have taken *ye* this afternoon, Mrs. Brodie? Now that Lady Ambersley's necklace has been found."

"I went to the Times this afternoon and spoke with Mr. Burke regarding an article he wrote for the crime sheet in this morning's edition. It seems he has a friend within the MET who contacted him after the call came in about the chief inspector's death."

"Aye? What did he share with ye?"

"It could be important to *our* inquiries into the murder of the chief inspector and perhaps Constable Martin."

That dark gaze narrowed as I gathered my bag and went to the door.

"I'll explain what I was able to learn on the ride to Scotland Yard."

Nine

NEW SCOTLAND YARD, THE
VICTORIA EMBANKMENT

ON THE RIDE to the Embankment, I explained what Mr. Burke had eventually shared due to subtle persuasion and a little assistance from Rupert, regarding the chief inspector looking for information about that old case.

"Blackwood," Brodie repeated the name with a frown. "It's been a long time since I heard the name."

"You worked on the case?"

He nodded. "Aye, with Joseph Martin. I had just made inspector, and he was the constable on duty when the poor young woman's body was found."

Our driver stopped before the main entrance of the "Yard" as it was called, what was now the main headquarters of the Metropolitan Police.

It was several stories tall, an imposing red-brick and stone building that was rumored to also include meeting rooms for high-ranking officials and offices for the growing Criminal Investigation Department.

That included Chief Inspector Abberline, and a morgue

where bodies were received for further inspection by medical professionals as part of a growing need for their services.

Personally, I considered there to be no difference between Abberline and bodies in the morgue.

He was quite despicable, incompetent, and not to be trusted, as noted by others as well as myself, and merely waiting out the time until his pension. It would come none too soon, as far as I was concerned.

A plain-clothed young man rose from his desk and greeted us as we entered the lobby.

"Yes, sir...madam," he added with a somewhat curious look at myself. "How may I assist you?"

Brodie handed him the note from the Home Secretary's office.

"And this would be in the matter of?" he inquired.

"The matter of the recent death of Chief Inspector Dawes," Brodie replied. "The body was brought here and is presently in the morgue."

The young man nodded. "And you are?"

"Angus Brodie and Lady Mikaela Forsythe, private consultants. I spoke with Inspector Dooley earlier.

"Of course. I will advise him that you have arrived."

We waited as the clerk, who was quite young, made a telephone call presumably to Mr. Dooley, who arrived promptly. He nodded in greeting.

"I've made the necessary arrangements for you to inspect the body." He indicated that we were to follow him.

"Perhaps the lady would care to wait in one of our private offices," the young clerk suggested.

"I assure you, the lady has no doubt seen more dead bodies than yourself, Mr. Davidson," Mr. Dooley informed him as we proceeded past what was referred to as the booking desk, down a long hallway past a meeting room where the meeting had just adjourned, then toward the part of the building opposite the embankment.

Constables and plain-clothed men emerged from the large room, including Chief Inspector Abberline, who immediately exchanged glances with Brodie, then stopped Mr. Dooley.

"As you well know, Mr. Dooley, the examination rooms are out of limits to the general public."

"Yessir, well aware. However, this is on direct orders from the office of the Home Secretary."

Mr. Dooley did not wait for a response but motioned for Brodie and me to follow him.

"I might say, a pleasure as always..." I said no more as we followed Mr. Dooley through a set of double doors with signage that noted a holding area and morgue with four private offices.

The door to one of the offices opened, and an older woman emerged with reddened eyes as she sniffled into her handkerchief. She was accompanied by an attendant who escorted her past as another door, much the same as in a hospital with a glass viewing window, opened. A man in a white bibbed apron emerged with a clipboard in hand and proceeded into another private office.

Mr. Dooley motioned for us to follow him. "This way, room number eight."

In spite of the fact that Brodie was no longer part of the MET, there was that note of respect in his voice.

"As you requested, I made certain the clothes be made available for you to inspect as well," he added as he held the door open, then nodded to an attendant.

"Dawes is the name," Mr. Dooley informed the attendant

with thick glasses, who was also dressed in a white bibbed apron.

He went to a wall with several compartments, opened one and pulled out an examination table with a sheet over.

I had seen a number of bodies since that first case with Brodie. It was the nature of the inquiry business that not all cases involved small four-legged thieves with a penchant for rubies and diamonds.

However...

There was always that initial reaction—a bit of shock quickly pushed aside with other matters of importance, and my own habit of quickly pressing on.

"And the clothes?" Brodie inquired.

"On the counter as requested," the attendant replied and indicated a long counter along the wall where men's garments had been laid out.

They included a shirt badly stained with what had to be blood, vest, jacket, trousers, a pair of men's undergarments, stockings, and boots.

"The body first," Brodie indicated, and the attendant swept the sheet back much like a magician about to reveal whether or not a body had disappeared.

It had not and gleamed under a series of overhead electric lights, skin a shade of white with a green tinge about the edges, dried blood on the throat and chest above a paunch of belly, and manly parts on full display.

"A little discretion in consideration of the lady," Mr. Dooley insisted, and the sheet was returned over the lower part of the chief inspector's body.

As Brodie made his inspection, the attendant proceeded to point out three wounds on the body, all around the throat and neck.

"One wound would have been sufficient to accomplish wot the murderer wanted," he commented.

I had taken out my notebook—that did seem to be a better alternative that viewing the chief inspector's naked body—and made note of Brodie's observations.

"And there are bruises about the neck as well..."

I made that note of that.

"And bruising about the ribs as if struck a blow with a boot after the man was down. And torn nails on the fingers."

I added that to the notes.

"Blotchy blue patches on the stomach," Brodie lifted the far edge of the sheet. "And on the upper right leg."

"I noticed that as well," Mr. Dooley commented.

I found his observations to be most interesting as I added yet another note.

He lowered the sheet back into place. "His clothes," he indicated and proceeded to the counter.

"As you see, the shirt is quite bloodied," the attendant pointed out. "Which is consistent with the wounds on the throat."

Brodie made no comment as he inspected each garment, making note of a stain on the left lapel of the jacket. He wiped a finger across the stain, then tasted it.

"Sticky and sweet," he commented as he exchanged a look with Mr. Dooley.

I added the note as he then continued his inspection, including the boots.

He picked up one then the other. "Smooth, no marks."

I had no idea what that might mean, but added it as well.

Brodie stood back from the counter, deep in thought, as he finished his inspection of the garments.

"That will be all," he said then and thanked the attendant for his assistance.

I returned my notebook to my bag, and we followed Mr. Dooley from the examination room, past other examination rooms and offices to the main entrance of the building.

"I will call on you later to discuss everything," Mr. Dooley informed us rather abruptly.

I then saw the reason for his hasty farewell as Chief Inspector Abberline rapidly made his way toward us.

One of the advantages of being very near the 'Yard' was that there were several coaches on the street, either arriving or departing. Brodie waved down a driver and we climbed inside.

"Are ye all right, lass?" Brodie asked as we departed Scotland Yard and Chief Inspector Abberline.

"The look on yer face was concernin' when the attendant first pulled back the sheet."

"Quite all right," I assured him.

I wasn't about to admit that it was a bit of a shock compared to other bodies I had seen in the past. Not so much the wounds, which were dreadful. Not surprising, considering the description Mr. Dooley provided, but other...things.

"Other things?" He inquired.

Oh, for heaven's sake!

"The poor man did seem a bit lacking in certain parts."

"Certain parts?" he repeated.

He was deliberately being difficult. I saw it in the amusement in that dark gaze.

"Manly parts," I blurted out, since it seemed he wouldn't be satisfied until I explained.

"And ye are an authority on this?" he commented with straight face.

He could be such a devil.

"I do appreciate that you are not similarly afflicted," I explained. "Although, perhaps it is a condition that sets in when one is dead."

He coughed through laughter and finally brought himself under control once more.

"I will remind ye of that, Mikaela Forsythe."

He continued to use my titled name when making a point.

"I look forward to it, Mr. Brodie."

It was late in the afternoon when we arrived back at the Strand. Neither of us had eaten, and the first order of business was early supper at the Public House.

The meat pie was delicious and warmed me through.

I chatted briefly with Miss Effie, now Mrs. Cavendish. She was a cheerful woman with round cheeks, eyes that sparkled, and a demeanor that tolerated no nonsense from her customers, the workers that arrived at end of day.

Mr. Cavendish had accompanied us, and presently made the rounds of those he knew, blocking the walk area with his platform, then moving on before putting in a take-away order for two pies: one for the hound.

"He gets right put out if I don't bring one back for him," he commented. "You spoilt him with that, Miss Mikaela."

"Surely not," I replied and had Brodie include the two take-away meals on our total.

After supper, we returned to the office. I poured us both a dram of Old Lodge whisky while Brodie built up the fire in the coal stove.

I handed him a glass, then opened my notebook and went to the chalkboard. I made a separate column for Brodie's observations of the chief inspector's body beside the list I had made earlier from the description in the police report for Constable Martin:

"The cut at the throat was the cause of death," I said as I made the note.

"Eventually."

I turned. Brodie had loosened the tie I had so expertly tied earlier.

"Eventually?"

"It was a slow wound."

"What about the blotchy blue patches?" I made another note. I had not seen that before on a body.

"It happens as the body is dying."

He said it in such a matter-of-fact manner, and I could only imagine other things he had seen in his time with the MET and before on the streets as a young boy.

"And the bruises along the ribs? It would seem that he was beaten as well."

"More like he was kicked after he went down."

Kicked? For what purpose since he was dying or already dead?

"What of the bruising on his neck in addition to the cut?" I then asked. "What would be the purpose of it with the other wounds?"

He replied with a single word.

"Rage."

I was momentarily taken aback, the only sound in the office the hiss of the kettle on the coal stove.

"His throat was cut, but he fought back. When he went down, he was viciously kicked—unnecessary as ye said," Brodie explained. "But it was more than that, far more. Whoever attacked him wanted to inflict as much pain and suffering as possible even as the man was dying."

"For what reason?" I asked.

"So that Chief Inspector Dawes would know."

What he described was horrible, almost beyond comprehension, such cruelty. As if...

"For revenge?" I whispered.

That dark gaze met mine. "Aye, revenge."

"Over what?"

A question for which there was no answer. At least not yet.

In spite of the fire in the coal stove that warmed the office, I was cold to the bone.

"What of the substance on the jacket?" I then asked.

"Morphine. I've seen it before."

"And his boots? You seemed most interested in them."

A faint smile. "Ye dinna miss anything."

"What were you looking for?"

"A mark I noticed in the ash on the floor before the hearth at the residence."

"What sort of mark?"

"The mark of a work boot."

"Worn by the murderer?"

He nodded. "Very possible. It would seem that whoever wore those boots was in that room with the Chief Inspector Dawes."

If there was more, he didn't share it. At least not now.

"It could be useful to follow the information our friend, Mr. Burke, provided."

"He is not a friend," I corrected him. "The only reason he is willing to provide information is because he sees how it might benefit himself, or under threat."

"I would imagine that ye managed that quite well."

"We do have an understanding," I admitted. "And he is quite put off by Rupert."

"What about the information he provided regarding inquiries the Chief Inspector Dawes was making? Might there be something there?"

He was thoughtful. "Perhaps."

I returned to the board and made additional notes from things we had discussed, still unable to rid myself of that cold feeling deep inside.

Two men had been murdered, their wounds and manner of death similar.

Were they connected? And for what reason had Chief Inspector Dawes inquired about a man by the name of Blackwood?

Was he working a case of his own, even though he was retired? Or did his death have nothing to do with the inquiries that Burke had assisted him with?

"Come away, lass. We'll not find the answers there tonight. I have inquiries I'll make in the morning. Perhaps I will learn something there from what Mr. Burke told ye."

I undressed in the adjacent room that had become our bedchamber then slipped into bed. The window glass rattled as the wind came up, and Brodie was there. He pulled me against him.

"Yer cold as ice," he commented as a warm hand moved over my shoulder then down my arm.

"Is that a complaint?" I replied.

"It's enough to put a man off."

He lay against my back, his arm about my waist, in that way that had become habit. A welcome habit that I reached for at the end of the day, my hand curled in his. Quite odd, I thought for someone who had decided she didn't need anyone.

I turned toward him.

"That's never bothered you before."

"Ye are a cheeky lass," he whispered.

~

It was late in the evening, the courts of the Old Bailey closed for the day, trials concluded, sentences handed out, as the last of those who worked inside completed their roles in the name of justice. Constables in dark blue uniforms, clerks, and judges leaving as the horde of cleaning people arrived at the entrance.

They carried the tools of their trade—sweepers, mops, buckets—for removing the dust and debris inside—the waste of human lives.

He crossed the street, his gait slower than it had once been, each step an effort as he joined them, melting in with the steady stream of men and women whose lives were bound to the Old Bailey, as his had been.

The inside of the Old Bailey was as he remembered it, plain and stark, adjoining Newgate prison, a cold reminder of his time there, a stone abomination of courts and judges' chambers.

There were four courtrooms as well as prisoners' cells and the dreaded 'Dead Man's Walk,' that stark passage that led to Newgate and the gallows.

He heard that it was all to be torn down, the prison along with it, and replaced by a new Court of Justice with far more courtrooms to handle cases.

A phalanx of constables watched as the cleaners gathered. They paid him no mind. He was simply one of many, there to do his work. Only his work was not to be found at the end of a sweeper, or mop and bucket.

He waited now as others departed in groups, an army of

nameless souls sent off to their assigned areas as he had once been nameless to those who watched.

There were four courtrooms on the main floor beyond the entrance hall, which included the judges' chambers and the private chamber for Judge E. L. Cameron, his name on the placard stand beside the door.

He had been there days before to make certain of it and also to make certain the judge still held court there. With a signature the judge had meted out his sentence, forever altering his life.

He had discovered that Judge Cameron often worked late —mustn't let the paperwork for a man's sentence linger. Cameron then departed well after workers and those who guarded the halls had left, with only a handful of constables who remained.

Judge Cameron was still there even now as he followed a handful of cleaning people. Head down with his cap pulled low, he glanced to those who watched and chatted, their attention distracted.

He abruptly left the group and turned down the adjacent hallway where those courtrooms were located, still and darkened, with the judges' rooms across, memory sharp as a blade.

It was perfect that it would be done here, where justice was handed out. Where he now handed out justice.

He listened at the door, then opened it, and stepped inside.

Judge Cameron sat at a desk across the room, features cast in shadows from the desk lamp as he studied papers before him, then a quick signature that no doubt sealed another man's fate.

The day's work obviously done, the judge set aside his pen, gathered the paperwork, and set it aside as well.

He had changed little in the years since, white hair perhaps thinner. Yet the firm set of the jaw, that he remembered so well, was still there. Resolute, determined.

The judge wore a black robe, that costume of 'justice.' He rose, removed it, then went to the small closet behind the desk.

This was the moment the man who moved through the shadows had waited for.

The judge struggled, fought, and tried to protect himself as he was slammed against the closet door then viciously turned about.

His fist closed around the front of the judge's shirt as he brought his other hand up, the knife gleaming in the light from the judge's desk.

"Twelve years…" his attacker hissed. "Day in and day out, the filth and disease, prisoners who kill over a crust of bread, and the sound of their screams as they're led to the gallows. I have waited.

"Now, I want you to feel what it is to know you are about to lose everything!" he told the judge as he drew the blade slowly across his throat, just enough to nick the vein there.

Judge Cameron, esteemed member of the courts for over thirty years, master of the pen that had condemned him, stared back incredulously as blood seeped from the wound and soaked the front of his coat.

"Who are you…?" The question suddenly died as he was lowered to the floor of his chambers.

"You!" he gasped, recognition dawning at last as he stared up at the man who stood over him. And then a last gurgling breath.

His murderer stepped back from the body. Labored breathing gave way to that painful cough.

It came more often now, and there was blood with it. It wouldn't be long now, but it would be long enough.

There was one more, and then it would be done...

Ten

THE PERSISTENT RINGING of the service bell brought us both up out of sleep, followed by the determined pounding at the office door.

Brodie cursed, first in Scots, then in the Queen's English, for whoever might be outside the door, as he grabbed his trousers, then wool jumper against the cold in the room.

"Who the bloody hell is it this time of the night?"

Actually, it was very near morning—very early morning to be specific with a glance at the faint edge of light on the window shade.

The pounding at the door continued, joined now by furious barking by the hound.

"Stay where it's warm, while I learn who it is needs to die this early in the mornin'," Brodie said as he left the room.

He was not serious, of course, still the sentiment was there. I reached for my pocket watch.

It was only half past five in the morning!

I thought of several reasons someone might be at the door that time of day, the first that something had happened with my great-aunt. At her age, I could never be certain how much longer she had, even though she was quite determined to outlive the Queen, and several other persons of her acquaintance, before boarding a Viking long boat into the great beyond.

That thought also included my sister and her family. What if it was some difficulty with the baby, Catherine, who was hardly an infant any longer?

My next thought, as I heard voices, was for my ward, Lily Montgomery, whom I had brought from Edinburgh as a child after one of our cases.

Although she was now very much an independent young woman who had a habit of taking herself off 'exploring,' as she called it. The last time it had been in my great-aunt's motor carriage for a drive about.

Munro had eventually learned the direction she had taken across London and proceeded to find her. It had not ended well for Munro, who was my aunt's estate manager. It was he who had discovered that the motor carriage was missing.

All had ended well enough several hours later when Lily returned with cheeks smudged with mud from the street, the expression in her eyes afire as she recounted her adventures to my great-aunt, who had eventually summoned me to Sussex Square to hear the tale.

"She is quite like yourself," she pointed out, not for the first time. While I struggled between thoughts of stern reprimand for someone who was now somewhere near nineteen or twenty years of age.

The alternative was choking back laughter at the memory of a similar incident of my own that involved my great-aunt's racehorse and an unauthorized turn about the racetrack at Ascot in full view of the Royal family.

Was it possible that Lily had taken off on another adventure and gotten herself into some difficulty?

I swung my legs over the edge of the bed as I recognized Mr. Dooley's thick Irish accent and the excitement in his voice.

I was hardly dressed for callers in my chemise and petticoat...still, this did seem urgent. I grabbed Brodie's dress coat from the chair back, wrapped it around me and went into the outer office.

"With all that's happened, I thought you should know straight away," Mr. Dooley was saying.

"Aye." Brodie replied.

"The same?" I heard him ask.

Mr. Dooley nodded. "The very same that Constable Martin was killed, and everyone at the courts in a fit and falling in the middle of it over how it could possibly have happened. They have brought on extra men and sent them across London.

"The thought is that it had to be someone who had good knowledge of the Old Bailey," he continued. "And that the judge would be found there after hours at end of day, when there would be fewer people about and it would be easier to move around. It's thought that he came in with the cleaners."

Rupert had pushed inside the entrance to the office. He had ceased barking as he recognized Mr. Dooley and now sat on the floor, head cocked, ears alert as if he understood every word.

Mr. Dooley looked over and nodded as I entered the office.

"Beg pardon for the intrusion."

"It is no bother, Mr. Dooley," I assured him.

He returned to his conversation with Brodie. "I'll be leading the inquiries since this began with the attack on

Constable Martin. Remember, whoever is behind this is clever and had specific targets, it would seem."

I caught the look that Brodie gave Mr. Dooley. He nodded and then left the office. It did seem there was a great deal more to their conversation—their voices low before I entered the room.

Brodie went to the coal stove and added more coal, his expression quite serious in that way I had seen before, his mouth drawn with a frown.

I took the pot from atop the stove and filled it from the faucet in the water closet that had been added adjacent to the bedchamber. A recent addition that was quite marvelous, as it was no longer necessary to go to the accommodation down the hall, as when I first made Brodie's acquaintance.

Or rather, re-acquaintance...

He was at his desk when I returned, the frown still there as he leaned back on the edge of his desk and stared at the chalkboard.

I set the pot on the stove and added coffee from the tin on the shelf above, an acquired accomplishment as my kitchen skills were somewhat limited. The silence after Mr. Dooley's departure was still there.

"It is quite early for Mr. Dooley to call," I commented in an attempt to learn the reason. Brodie was usually more forthcoming.

"And by his manner it would seem quite serious. Oh, very well."

There was still no response as the pot on the stove began to bubble and hiss.

I let it bubble and hiss for a while, as I was quite familiar with his habit of pulling within himself when there was a matter that troubled him. There was no doubt this was the case now, considering the expression on his face, deep in thought.

Bubble and hiss, bubble and hiss. The smell of coffee along with the fire in the stove pushed back the chill in the office.

When it seemed that the pot had sufficiently completed its task, I picked up the towel for such things, seized the pot by the handle, and poured coffee in both our cups.

I returned the pot to the top of the stove where it continued to bubble once more, then took a cup to the brooding man who stood before the chalkboard, lost in thought as he stared at the notes I had made.

"I should dress in something more appropriate than my chemise and underdrawers if Mr. Dooley should return," I commented. "He was apparently somewhat embarrassed to see me in my bare feet and your coat."

There was a brief glance, clearly distracted, as Brodie took the cup, and then sipped the steaming coffee.

There was a sudden intake of breath.

"Is the coffee lacking?" I inquired, staring at him over the edge of my own cup.

I now had his full attention. He coughed, that dark gaze narrowed.

"Ye might have used a bit more coffee than necessary," he commented, barely more than a whisper.

"It serves you right—there was an opportunity for you to see to it as usual. You know full well that my skills in such things are quite lacking."

"I could stand up a spoon in it," he replied, somewhat stronger now.

"It is not that bad." I proceeded to take a sip and nearly choked. "Perhaps a bit stronger than your usual." I set my cup on the desk.

"Will you now tell me the reason Mr. Dooley was here?"

He took another sip of coffee. Brave man, I thought. I did need to pay attention to his skill in such things if we were both to survive.

He set his cup on the desk. Most unusual. He was in the habit of drinking a substantial amount of coffee in the morning, even if a spoon might have stood up in it. He went through our bedchamber into the adjoining water closet, and I heard the faint sound of water as it entered the basin.

He was most efficient in his morning wash and brush-up and set the tooth powder back on the shelf above the basin. Yet that dark beard glistened faintly with drops of water that remained as the towel was hastily tossed aside.

That dark gaze met mine, a different expression in the shadows that I was familiar with.

"There has been another murder."

He returned to the bedchamber and proceeded to dress for the day—a black jumper in place of the shirt, heavy socks with the boots, jerking the laces taut.

"I'll need my jacket," he said, matter of fact, as if he was setting off on some simple errand, for coffee perhaps, as I handed it to him, which left me standing in my chemise and underdrawers.

There was another expression that filled that dark gaze before he abruptly returned to the outer office.

He went to his desk and retrieved his revolver from the right-hand drawer, carefully checked it as he always did, then thrust it into his pocket.

I returned to the office as well. There was more to that startling announcement, and I was determined to hear it.

He had donned the cap he wore when the weather

demanded it, that dark gaze meeting mine again with the same expression that I'd glimpsed only moments before.

"Who...?" I started to ask, only to have the question silenced as he kissed me.

It was not the same as the night before, but gentle, with some thought that lingered unspoken as his breath met mine. And then he was gone, and I was left standing in my chemise and underdrawers.

"Oh, bloody hell."

While I knew nothing about the latest development in the case Brodie was pursuing, I did have information from my visit with Mr. Burke, a name that someone I knew might have knowledge of.

I quickly dressed, seized my long coat along with my travel bag that contained my notebook, then locked the office door behind me.

"Did Mr. Brodie say where he was off to?" I inquired of Mr. Cavendish as I reached the alcove by the street.

"I did overhear him tell the driver that he needed to get to the law courts at the Old Bailey."

Most interesting.

"Will you be needing a driver as well, Miss Mikaela?"

Mr. Jarvis had just come on shift. Mr. Cavendish waved him down and he pulled to a stop at the curb.

He tipped his cap. "Mornin', miss. A fine day to be out and about," he announced with a fair amount of sarcasm as icy rain turned to snow. "Where will it be this mornin'?"

"Sussex Square, Mr. Jarvis."

"And will the hound be joinin' you?"

Said hound was not to be seen.

"He's been out all night," Mr. Cavendish informed. "He'll

be a bit out of sorts and no good to anyone when he returns until he's had a nap."

With that, I climbed into the coach.

I discovered rather early on that my great-aunt was an astonishing source of information about a great many things. As she once commented, no one could live as long as she had without learning some very interesting and delicious things about the class she had been born into.

"I find people most interesting, particularly those of the upper class: quite pretentious and not above committing certain transgressions, including some of the most delicious scandals, unlike those of the lower class who make no pretense what they are about.

"Not that we haven't had our own share of scandals."

I had learned about some of those scandals after our great-aunt took my sister and me to live with her, following the scandal our father had created before his demise in the horse barn by his own hand. A scandal that left us each with the dresses we wore and little else after he gambled away the family fortunes that included our family home.

In the aftermath, I had vowed to never attach myself to a man. I had succeeded quite successfully in that until...Brodie.

"Good morning, Miss Mikaela!"

I had not bothered to telephone my great-aunt before leaving the office on the Strand and was met with more than a little surprise at the entrance to Sussex Square by Mr. Symons, her head butler.

"Good morning. Is Aunt Antonia up and about?"

Both my sister and I had long ago taken to referring to her as such, as most of the servants at Sussex had been with her longer than ourselves and were very much like our family as well.

"She was in the solar earlier, attempting to coax the sun out on this very cold, miserable morning. However, I believe she has removed to the small parlor, as she had one of the footmen light a fire in the fireplace."

I thanked him and made my way to the 'small' parlor, which was somewhat of a misnomer.

The original Sussex Square had been a royal fortress for William of Normandy, our esteemed ancestor, who ransacked most of England and declared himself king. He had lived here a short while before returning to France and other ransacking endeavors.

Over the centuries, several ancestors had torn down, then rebuilt various parts of Sussex Square, including the wall that surrounded it and the original medieval fortress.

More recently, as centuries went by, the manor that my sister and I had come to had been enlarged with the present Georgian manor that adjoined the medieval fortress with a very long hallway lit only by torches.

I knew it well as I had explored it in one of my early adventures. I had become lost in the old fortress and not found my way back until Aunt Antonia had found me.

"I became quite lost as a child myself," she explained. "It is a rather daunting pile of stones, particularly the dungeon. Remember to just keep climbing up."

Of course. So very simple—up.

I found her in the small parlor, the room embellished with tapestries on the wall and a portrait of her father who had one child, a daughter to whom he passed on notable family wealth and eccentricities.

The latter seemed to have missed a generation or two. However, Brodie would undoubtedly have argued the point.

"Good morning, dear," Aunt Antonia greeted me as well. "Have I forgotten some event? Was there a note? Or did you ring me up?"

I apologized for arriving without prior notice.

"Ah, a matter with some urgency. Is Mr. Brodie with you? I shall have Cook prepare breakfast for him. Men are always about food, or...as I have said, they live their lives between their stomachs and their manly parts. That's all, nothing more. Except perhaps Brodie."

She was quite fond of him.

"It is regarding information about someone for one of our inquiry cases."

"I am always pleased to assist in any way that I can. Do sit down."

She rose from her chair, royal as any queen, resplendent in satin as she went to the side table and poured a second cup of coffee. She handed it to me as I sat in the chair opposite.

"Now, tell me dear, how may I be of assistance?"

"What can you tell me about Sir Edward Blackwood?"

There was a very long pause, and then she set her cup on the table between our chairs.

"Sir Edward Blackwood, Viscount Lindhurst," she replied. "A nasty bit of business that was.

"There was a duel, as I remember." She was thoughtful as she poured what appeared to be a bit of whisky into her coffee. "A man once fought a duel over me. I realize you might find that difficult to believe."

I did not. There were several portraits of my great-aunt around Sussex Square. She was quite striking as a young woman. And still, I thought.

"Quite romantic for some," she continued. "However, I thought it was foolishness. He lost an ear in the process—the man who fought a duel over my honor." She smiled. "Not romantic at all."

Duels hadn't been fought for some time. At least not that were written up in the dailies. I was aware that most people considered them to be outdated, a dreadful part of the past, and prohibited in most places with legal consequences.

"What do you remember about it?"

"It seems there were financial difficulties. He had bet heavily in the hope of recouping enough to pay debts..." She paused and then apologized. "I'm sorry dear, no need to dredge up bad memories."

It was a familiar scenario that had led to my own father's disgrace and eventual suicide. That was when Aunt Antonia had stepped in and taken on two young girls when she was well past sixty years of age.

"No need to apologize," I assured her, then asked her to continue. "What happened?"

"There was a nasty confrontation with one of the gentlemen he owed a substantial amount. The man died and Sir Blackwood fled. The Metropolitan was called into it. As I remember, Brodie was newly made inspector then and pursued the case."

Brodie? An early case?

"The coffee is quite delightful with a wee dram," she suggested.

"Perhaps later," I replied. "You were saying?" I needed to know more.

"Blackwood was eventually caught, no doubt through Mr. Brodie's efforts. There was a trial. He was found guilty by the court and sent to prison." She added a bit more whisky to her coffee.

"A nasty affair."

Retired Chief Inspector Dawes had gone to Burke for any information that might be found about Blackwood. For a book he may have hoped to write about his time with the Metropolitan, as Burke thought, that included that trial?

Or for another reason?

I remained at Sussex Square and took breakfast with Aunt Antonia and Lily. It usually reminded me of when I was somewhat younger than Lily and the lively conversations at the breakfast table with my aunt and sister.

Then, as now, there were lively conversations. That was particularly true with Lily, determined for her own adventures, quite adamant that she didn't care to go to Paris as my sister Linnie and I had.

The last supper shared, Lily had been steadfast in her campaign to take the motor carriage out and about London. I had strongly spoken against it as a young lady out and about, alone, could be an easy target for mischief.

For her part, Lily had pointed out the knife she now carried, given to her by Munro, who had previously provided me with one as well that I carried inside my boot when out and about.

"She should be quite all right," Aunt Antonia had assured me. "She has been taking lessons at the gymnasium where you have spent some time, I believe, dear."

I had been overruled then, and she had taken herself out and about with no mishap. Brodie had pointed out at the time that he was far more concerned for anyone she might have encountered.

Munro had been against that adventure as well. I had

learned only afterward that there had been strong words between him and Lily over the matter.

According to Aunt Antonia, she was certain she overheard Lily tell him to *'bog off,'* apparently a term well-known among Scots.

When I had questioned Brodie about it afterward, he had choked, then laughed until I was certain there were tears in his eyes. He then explained the polite version of the phrase.

"The best way to explain would be that it means *'go away,'* although most usually with other less cordial words with it."

It did seem as if her time in England had not completely transformed Lily from the somewhat wild, independent-minded girl I had first met in Edinburgh. Not that I would have changed that about her even if it was possible, which it obviously was not.

I had to admit that even now I smiled at the memory of that particular episode.

Brodie often said that Lily and I were very much alike. Birds of a feather, as it were. However, this particular morning, she was unusually quiet and ate very little, then asked to be excused from the table.

"Of course, dear," Aunt Antonia replied.

When Lily had left the dining room, she then explained, "She has been somewhat withdrawn the last few days, not her usual self, since she received a post from Edinburgh."

Lily had left Edinburgh, as there was nothing left for her there after her place of employment, as a maid, had burned, leaving her homeless as well as without a source of income.

She had assisted Brodie and me with an inquiry case at the time, and I might have found myself in great difficulty if not for her resourcefulness. I had grown quite fond of her and proposed that she come to London as my ward. That included a place to live, an education, which was sorely lacking, and the possibility of a better future than a brothel in Edinburgh.

Intelligent, wise beyond her years, stubborn and brave, she had accepted my offer. In the years since, she had acquired an education, become a member of our somewhat unusual family, with a keen intelligence, a wicked sense of humor, and a penchant for speaking her mind.

She had been a challenge for Aunt Antonia, who insisted that she live at Sussex Square. Or perhaps the other way round. They were like two peas in a pod, and my great-aunt adored her.

Our conversations were usually about Lily's latest accomplishments or adventures, such as becoming lost in the old fortress, or taking herself off in the motor carriage. But I had noticed that she was especially quiet.

"Did she say who the post was from?" I inquired.

"Not a word."

I was aware that she received posts from time to time from a couple of the 'ladies' she had once worked for.

She had shared those with me, yet there had been no mention of one this morning.

"She did seem quite distracted by it," Aunt Antonia commented.

I hadn't spent a great amount of time with Lily and decided to look in on her before I left.

She was not in her bedchamber. I followed a familiar sound and found her in the Sword Room. The sound was her rather aggressive practice with one of our ancestors' weapons, a very fine rapier that I had used in the past.

I waited beside the mat Aunt Antonia had acquired for my practices with the blade as Lily parried, thrust several times at the target which was a large bag of sand suspended from the ceiling to recreate an opposing duelist.

Of course, it was less of a challenge than a living opponent, as the bag of sand did not strike back but instead swayed back and forth as sand fell from a series of 'wounds' that she had inflicted.

She parried and thrust once more, then returned to the beginning stance, somewhat out of breath. I did wonder who her 'opponent' might have been with all of those cuts.

I was certain she had no idea I was there until she turned, hazel-green eyes darkened from the intense 'battle' she had just finished.

"You've much improved," I complimented her. "It could be dangerous if I were to challenge you."

She gradually returned from wherever it was in her mind she had gone, driving that blade, absent the cork tip, into the target over and over again.

"I have had a very good instructor." She complimented me on the hundreds of hours we had shared in a mock duel, familiarizing her with the weight of the rapier, then the various moves that I had learned.

She had then spent hours more at the gymnasium, training with one of their instructors well-schooled in that ancient discipline, after it seemed she had far exceeded my ability to teach her more.

And now, where was it that she had gone as she quite furiously attempted to 'kill' the sandbag?

I went to that bag and inspected it. It was not the one we had last practiced with, but had obviously been replaced, no doubt after the demise of the previous one.

She stood apart, hands folded over the hilt of the rapier as if at the ready.

"I've decided I do not want to go to Paris," she announced with a side glance in my direction. "Mr. Munro said that I am an ungrateful *amadán*. It means 'fool' to the Scots."

I was somewhat familiar with the word.

It was obvious that she was waiting for something similar from me, but as I had in the past, I saw too much of myself in the young woman who stood before me as if prepared to do battle.

Willful, headstrong might be a better word, most certainly intelligent, and with wounds of her own from her earlier years in Edinburgh.

Then, before I could respond, as if she was afraid of what I might say, she asked, "How did you feel about what happened with your father?"

I added 'direct' to the list of qualities. However, that was part of who she was.

She knew somewhat about my early losses, a brief conversation we had when she first arrived from Scotland, but not about what I had felt at the time.

I did suppose this, too, was part of sharing my family with her—questions with difficult answers, much as I had asked them of my great-aunt.

She had not swept them under the rug as others would, preferring not to discuss difficult 'family' matters, but had been quite direct.

I had not perished from the answers but chose to believe that I was strengthened by 'difficult truths,' as she called them. Quite remarkable actually, and one of the many reasons that I adored my great-aunt.

I did understand that Lily being my ward, as it were, was more than a proper education, finishing school in Paris, proper dress, and proper manners.

How now to respond was the question. I would not simply sweep her decision to forego Paris under the carpet as a foolish notion.

"I was quite young at the time," I began, going back through the pages of memory. "I encountered many new things, different ways of looking back on what had happened, new experiences.

"I learned that I was strong, stronger than what had happened. I also learned that I could make my own way, be my own person, make my own decisions. I suppose that I have Aunt Antonia to blame for that."

There was a faint smile.

"She has said the same," she replied.

"You are a great deal like her," I said then, as I caught the pensive expression on her face. "With your own strengths and qualities."

"And you, as well?"

"I suppose she has been a strong influence," I admitted.

"Then you are not angry about my decision?"

"The first of many, I suspect. I must admit that it might be far easier if you were a meek creature who simply said 'yes, ma'am.' However, you are not, nor could you ever be. I knew that when we were escaping the Vaults beneath Edinburgh."

She was still quite serious. "I didn't want to disappoint you, after everything you've done for me."

"Now you are being a foolish chit."

The first of more conversations, I hoped, as I braved the rapier and gave her a strong embrace.

"What do you think of Madame Sybille?"

That certainly took the conversation in a different direction. Madame Sybille was the spiritualist and medium my great-aunt had brought to Sussex Square for her ladies' group.

"She seems to be quite entertaining," I replied. "Aunt Antonia is fond of her. She insists that she's very talented. As I recall, Madame Sybille helped one of her acquaintances find a ring her late husband had given her after it was lost. A good guess, no doubt."

"No doubt," Lily replied.

I sensed there might be more, however did not press the matter. From my own experience and knowing Lily as I did, I was certain there would be more conversations. She was most curious about things.

"I would like to practice a bit longer," she said then.

Of course, I thought as I left her to the demise of the sandbag.

"You have spoken with her?" Aunt Antonia inquired as I returned to the hall and collected my coat and umbrella. I nodded.

"It is remarkable how very much like myself she is, when I was that age."

"No adventure to the Greek Isles?"

"Nor to Paris it seems," I replied. "She has decided that she will not go."

My great-aunt smiled. "Interesting, though I am not surprised. She does have a mind of her own."

After leaving Sussex Square, I returned to the office at the Strand. Brodie had not yet returned from wherever he had gone with Mr. Dooley.

I straightened the bedroom as we had both left somewhat hastily, then the outer office as well.

There were notes I had made on the board regarding the Ambersley case, but only a handful regarding Brodie's inquiries after learning of Constable Martin's death.

The morning paper from the day before, with that article

on the crime sheet about the death of retired Chief Inspector Dawes, lay on my desk. I read what Burke had written again. It was brief.

It noted that retired former C.I. Dawes had succumbed to injuries of a suspicious nature and was found by his housekeeper at his residence in Hammersmith. The Metropolitan Police were subsequently contacted, and a constable was posted to the residence.

I tucked the newspaper into my bag, put on my long coat against the rain, and seized my umbrella from the stand beside the door.

~

BRODIE

He crouched down beside the body and made a cursory inspection of the wound there, with his pen lifting the collar of the judge's shirt.

A single wound there, barely more than a nick of a blade. But it was enough to open the vein causing the gradual death that followed, the judge's eyes staring blindly after the horror that had been visited upon him.

That wasn't all of it, though.

"The right hand," Mr. Dooley informed. "Almost as if…"

Brodie knew what he was about to say as he lifted the right arm, already stiffening and heavy with the rigor mortis that had begun to set in.

The fingers on the left hand had been severed, then placed on the desk on a court document by a folder that lay open, as the judge had apparently worked early before the courts opened.

"Aye," Brodie replied.

Revenge. The word was there, the murder most definitely meant to send a message.

The judges' chambers, including the entire courts, might have been closed off to anyone except members of the MET and CID.

Mr. Dooley had informed the constables posted at the entrance that Brodie was to be allowed access, authorized by the Home Secretary.

A bit of a stretch of the truth, yet perhaps not.

Another murder. The judge very clearly left to slowly bleed to death as the killer went about his grim task with that display on the desk.

A message? Or merely the final step in his task.

Three murders within a matter of days. And all the victims were known to Brodie from his time with the MET.

Eleven

HAMMERSMITH, LONDON

MIKAELA

I WAS NOT surprised to see a plain-clothed man at the entrance to the residence of Chief Inspector Dawes.

In working with Brodie on other inquiry cases that eventually included the Metropolitan Police, I'd learned it was not unusual to find an inspector stationed at the scene of a crime. Particularly if the crime involved someone of some stature.

In this case, it was the murder of one of their own, so to speak, even though the chief inspector had been retired for several years.

The inspector nodded as I stepped down from the coach and approached the front entrance. I did not recognize him.

He held up a hand. "Sorry, miss. The residence is restricted due to an incident. Do you have business here?"

I had prepared for this without Brodie accompanying me. I retrieved one of our calling cards from my bag and handed it to him.

"Angus Brodie and Mikaela Forsythe, Private Inquiries?" he read the front of the card.

I nodded. "We have been given authority in the matter by the Home Secretary. Mr. Brodie is to meet me here. I do hope you won't keep me waiting in the rain."

A bit of a stretch of the truth, as Brodie was not aware that I had decided to come there.

"The Home Secretary, you say?"

"Due to the victim's long service with the MET, we are assisting in the investigation."

Admittedly, a somewhat thinly disguised excuse, as we had not officially been requested to participate. Still...

"Very well. I'll not keep you waiting in this beastly weather. You may go inside, but don't disturb anything within the premises. There's no one about, the housekeeper has made other arrangements."

I thanked him. "I am here to observe and make notes of the scene." I had come prepared for that part of it and held my notebook aloft.

"Tedious work at times," I added. "However, quite necessary even though I am certain your people have been quite thorough."

He nodded from under his brimmed hat, then opened the door for me.

The foyer of the residence contained a coat rack with umbrella stand, a long coat hanging from the rack, where the chief inspector or perhaps his housekeeper had placed it after he returned from some outing. Nothing unusual in that.

I inspected the door. There were no scrape marks or other indication that the murderer had forced his way in from that direction.

Was the murderer known to the chief inspector and he had

let him in? Or had he entered the residence by some other means?

According to Mr. Dooley, the housekeeper heard no sounds to indicate what she found in the front parlor afterward.

I went in search of some other means the murderer might have gained entrance.

It was a modest residence on a street with other similar residences of people of modest means, yet neatly kept, no doubt due to the efforts of the housekeeper who found the chief inspector's body.

I turned on the electric, then slowly walked through the small dining area attached to the kitchen, a room that would have been for the housekeeper, and a second access just beyond at the back of the residence.

Once again, there was no sign that someone had forced their way inside, along with the fact that the housekeeper had seen no one.

I returned to the foyer and the small hall that led to the stairs to the second floor, as well as the front parlor where the body was found.

According to Mr. Dooley, it didn't appear that anything had been taken. However, a more thorough search with the aid of the housekeeper was to be made.

If nothing was taken, then that would eliminate robbery as the motive for the murder.

Unless, of course, the chief inspector had come upon the murderer unexpectedly before he could take anything.

I was careful not to touch anything as I entered the modestly furnished room and once again turned on the electric in order to make my own observations.

It was simply furnished with a rug over the wood floor, an

overstuffed chair that sat before the hearth with a small table beside, and a humidor and pipe in a tray.

My attention was immediately drawn to the floor before the hearth and the dark stain on the carpet, where the chief inspector's body had been found.

The rug was scuffed up at the edge as if the toe of a boot might have caught it. The murderer perhaps, or his victim as he struggled while he was attacked?

I crossed to the narrow windows adjacent to the hearth. There was a faint scrape in the wood of the window casement.

Was it possible that was the means the murderer had made his way inside, and then attacked the chief inspector?

I glanced back at the entrance to the parlor and the small dining room and kitchen beyond. It was quite possible the housekeeper wouldn't have heard the window being opened.

A copy of the police report might tell us more.

I continued my search as I approached the desk that sat across from the hearth.

According to Burke at the Times, the chief inspector had contacted him for information regarding an old case that Burke had written about several years before.

"Perhaps writing a book about his time with the MET," Burke had suggested, amused by the thought.

I went to the desk, disappointed that I had not discovered anything out of the ordinary that might provide a clue to the reason Chief Inspector Dawes was so brutally murdered.

There were the usual things I would expect to find, familiar from my own writing endeavors. Pen, writing paper, envelopes, perhaps for correspondence, and a folder that clearly held other papers. Not unusual either for a man who had worked for over twenty years as inspector for the MET, then several more as Chief Inspector.

According to Brodie and Mr. Dooley, the man was highly respected and undoubtedly would have received many accolades and commendations, and perhaps certificates of recognition.

Was that what was inside that folder? Or was the chief inspector conducting an investigation of his own with those inquiries he'd made of Burke?

Brodie has often said that, for a woman, I have an unusual curiosity for things that have led to some interesting, even dangerous situations.

My great-aunt prefers to call it a keen intellect, along with a somewhat stubborn nature.

I should undoubtedly leave the folder undisturbed as the man with the MET at the entrance had reminded me.

I should simply make a note of it. Those in charge of the case for the MET might be able to investigate further, and perhaps had already and discovered there was nothing there of importance...

Yes, well, as I had also learned from Brodie, it was often the smallest detail that provided information that led to the resolution of a case.

I listened for any sound that the man at the door might have followed to check on me. I heard nothing, opened my bag, and took out my writing pen. Mindful of leaving any trace that might be found by those investigating the case for the MET, I used the pen to lift the front edge of the folder.

There were several pages of notes, a crime report dated ten years earlier, and an official looking letter from the Prison Commission.

The notes were brief, much the same that I had seen Brodie write. Dates, with a half-dozen words at most for each to describe something he apparently was most interested in, a yellowed police report that he had kept or persuaded someone within the MET to provide. The name in the report...Edward Blackwood.

A book in progress, perhaps. Or something else?

There was more as I carefully shifted the report aside and discovered a formal letter dated only a matter of ten days earlier, from the Prison Commission, signed by the chairman of the commission. I leaned closer to read the contents of the letter that was addressed to the chief inspector.

This letter is to inform you of a situation that has
recently occurred.
On 6 January of this year, it was noted that a prisoner
referred to hospital for a medical condition
has in fact escaped and left hospital.
You are advised in the matter as the prisoner was
originally brought into custody through your efforts and others of
the Metropolitan Police.
The prisoner in question is considered dangerous. All efforts
will be made to return him to prison.

It was signed by the Commissioner of Prisons, and the last line of the letter—

The prisoner's name? Edward Blackwood!

Had Chief Inspector Dawes decided to conduct his own investigation after receiving that letter?

It did seem that the chief inspector's inquiries were not for a book he was writing, but an effort to find Blackwood.

Inspectors with the MET had already made a cursory inspection of the residence according to Mr. Dooley. Yet, that folder with that letter remained.

If Mr. Dooley knew of it, he would surely have told Brodie.

The Commission had chosen to contact Chief Inspector Dawes directly.

Was it to keep the matter out of the newspapers so as not to cause difficulty for the MET, which had suffered failures in other investigations? Or to protect the citizens of London?

What would happen once the folder was inspected by those investigating the murder of the chief inspector?

Would it simply be swept under the carpet, as Brodie indicated had happened in the past with cases that were considered too sensitive, or too dangerous for the citizens of London to know about?

I heard a sound from the front entrance of the residence. No doubt the inspector come to check upon me.

I quickly made my decision and stuffed the letter into my bag.

"Lady Forsythe?" the inspector inquired as he appeared at the entrance to the parlor.

"It seems that Mr. Brodie may have been delayed."

"It does indeed."

I thanked him and quickly left before any questions could be asked.

When I arrived at the Strand, Mr. Cavendish rolled out from the alcove in spite of the downpour of rain that had set in.

"Rupert is not about?" I inquired as I paid the driver and made my way into the shelter of the alcove.

"Took himself off toward the Public House a bit earlier."

"Has Mr. Brodie returned?" I glanced toward the windows on the second-floor landing.

"A short while ago with Mr. Dooley. Took themselves up to the office in a bit of a hurry and without a word, like before a storm out at sea."

And I did suppose that Mr. Cavendish should know, as he had spent a good many years aboard ship at sea before the accident that took his legs.

Had there been a development regarding the murder of Constable Martin or Chief Inspector Dawes?

I thought of the letter I had discovered and turned toward the lift.

"It's not working at present, Miss Mikaela," Mr. Cavendish informed me. "A bit of water might have gotten into the electric."

I thanked him as I turned toward the stairs that led to the second-floor landing and the office.

"A bit of caution, miss. Mr. Brodie asked where you were and didn't much care for the answer when I told him you didn't say."

I had not left a note.

"It's just that he worries about you." He gave me a wink. "It seems to be a common affliction. I worry about my Effie when she takes a notion to go out and about on her own."

I thanked him again for the warning and made a quick dash up the stairs.

Hadn't cared for Mr. Cavendish's answer seemed to be an understatement, as I entered the office and was met with a dark glare.

"What is it?" I inquired. "Has something happened?"

The two men exchanged a look. Brodie said nothing.

"There's been another murder," Mr. Dooley replied.

"Where?"

"At the law courts, one of the judges, Judge Cameron, was

found murdered in his chambers early this morning before others arrived."

There were dozens of questions.

How was it possible someone was able to get inside?

Were there any suspects?

Three murders in less than a handful of days?

I remembered the letter and retrieved it from my bag. I handed it to Mr. Dooley.

"From the Commissioner of Prisons? How did you come by this?" He handed the letter to Brodie.

"That is somewhat difficult to explain." I deliberately avoided looking at Brodie.

"Perhaps ye better explain."

There was something in Brodie's voice, something different than the usual frustration at something I had done without making him aware.

"After what I learned from Mr. Burke at the Times, it seemed there could be something important to be learned regarding inquiries the chief inspector had made, almost as if he was conducting his own investigation into a certain matter.

"I went to his residence..." I didn't mention that the inspector on duty had been most accommodating.

"I was able to go inside. I found the letter in a folder on the desk. The name was the same as the name Mr. Burke had provided. It seemed important."

There was more, but I did not go into further explanation.

"Blackwood," Mr. Dooley repeated the name with a look across at Brodie.

There was that irritating look between them once more. While it did seem that I had discovered something important, it could be most off-putting. Particularly when Mr. Dooley made no explanation, but instead pocketed the letter, then retrieved his hat and umbrella.

He exchanged another look with Brodie as he turned to leave. "We have every extra man on this, but it may not be enough."

"Aye."

Silence filled the office after he left.

The anger that was there when I first returned was gone, hidden behind the mask of the police investigator he had once been.

"Was that letter important?" I asked. It very much seemed that it was. "What did Mr. Dooley mean that it may not be enough? What do you know about Blackwood?"

He did not reply straight away. Instead, he went to the cabinet and retrieved a bottle of Old Lodge whisky, then poured us both a dram and then one more.

He told me of that old case with Blackwood, the details very much the same as my great-aunt had remembered them, a sad, pathetic story that might have come from my own childhood. Except that it had ended in murder.

Brodie was the investigator assigned to the case. Days became weeks, but Blackwood was eventually found with the aid of someone Brodie had worked with before, Constable Martin, who had donned plain clothes and searched the streets, back alleys, and brothels with him.

They followed every clue, even the ones that revealed nothing, until they were able to find Blackwood.

Retired Chief Inspector Dawes had written up the charges for Blackwood and had him taken to the old Scotland Yard, where he was imprisoned until his trial. Judge Cameron presided over Blackwood's trial at the Old Bailey and handed down his sentence.

Blackwood's lawyer at the time had argued the encounter was self-defense. In view of the uncertainty of premeditated malice against the victim, Blackwood had been sentenced to thirty years in prison.

Twelve years before. And now Blackwood had managed to escape.

The reality of what that meant was horrifying. Three of four people directly responsible for his capture, conviction, and imprisonment were now dead.

I expected angry words over my visit to the chief inspector's residence. Brodie surprised me.

"Ye cannot be a part of this."

Not be part...!

It caught me off-guard, unprepared when I thought I knew exactly, or very near, what he would have said.

"I can help you find Blackwood," I informed him. "Haven't I already demonstrated that with the letter? And you cannot possibly do this alone..."

"No, lass. Ye dinna know the places I will go. And I willna be alone."

Munro. Of course. Who knew the streets of London better?

Still, when I would have objected further, he pulled me to him, a hand gentle on my cheek.

"I need ye here for any information Mr. Dooley may be able to learn from his men on the street. Mr. Cavendish can get word to me if ye learn something important." He brushed a strand of hair back from my cheek. "That is how ye best help me in this."

I didn't argue the point.

"I would have yer promise that ye will not take yerself off again as ye did today."

I reluctantly nodded.

"I would hear ye say it."

Bloody hell.

"If you will promise to send word that you are still alive out there," I countered.

He smiled, wicked man.

"I promise."

Twelve

WE STAYED the night at the office once again.

I rose early with Brodie as he prepared to leave.

"Did Blackwood have a family in London? Might they have heard from him?" I inquired as he dressed.

He gave me a long look, a reminder of our conversation the previous evening. I went into the outer office.

There was a scratching at the door, and I let the hound in. He immediately went to warm himself near the fire in the stove that Brodie had set when we first rose.

The hound was most amicable, most of the time. He did like Brodie, when he had food that could be beggared. However, he had his other moments.

I slipped him a biscuit, left from the previous day. He was not some miniature, yapping nuisance and could be quite intimidating. He was my insurance against any argument regarding that conversation the night before.

"Good boy," I told him as he inhaled the biscuit then went to lie before the firebox.

"What of your conversation with Mr. Brown? He is usually well informed and has been a reliable source in the past."

I looked up, uneasy at the somewhat obvious silence as Brodie came into the outer office. "I promised to assist from here if there should be word. I did not promise that I wouldn't ask questions."

"Ye must remind me to be more specific next time."

I didn't bother to acknowledge that.

"As to your question, I have spoken with Mr. Brown. He will get word to me when he learns something about Blackwood. The man seems to have a need for morphine; however, having fled the hospital, he'll have only what he can steal."

"What were you forced to promise in exchange for his assistance?"

"Ah lass, ye doubt me. It is himself that owes me the favor."

And not the first time I had heard that. I did wonder about their 'working relationship;' however, I had learned not to ask too many questions about it.

Part of the things, Brodie informed me, it would be best that I didn't know about.

"When will I hear from you?" I asked instead as he donned his thick worsted coat and billed cap, even though I already knew the answer.

That was the complicated part of working apart, particularly in a situation that was more than merely following up on information as in the case of a missing necklace.

"Mr. Dooley will be working the case from the MET. I will send word round to Mr. Cavendish."

Which translated to...maybe, perhaps if possible, or 'yes dear.'

"Might someone from the Agency be of help?"

He shook his head. "Best to keep this away from the Agency if possible."

I understood the reasons.

"I was thinking there might be something to learn from the hospital," I suggested.

"It would be easy enough to inquire. Mr. Dooley would have information for that. It could be useful."

I smiled as I looked over at him.

"Aye, perhaps."

It was a compromise of sorts. Rather than sitting on my hands, so to speak.

"If ye learn something important, give it to Mr. Cavendish. He'll find Mr. Brown and get it to me. And yer to take the hound with ye."

"Of course, dear."

There was that smile just at one corner of his mouth.

He checked the revolver and put it in his coat pocket, and then he was gone, down the stairs with a final word to Mr. Cavendish, then across the street until he disappeared.

I added notes regarding the case to the chalkboard and frowned as I read the names of the three persons who had been murdered: Constable Martin, Chief Inspector Dawes, retired, and Magistrate Judge Cameron.

Three of four men responsible all those years before for catching Edward Blackwood after that horrific incident, bringing him to trial, finding him guilty, and then sentencing him to prison.

And yet there remained one more man who had led the investigation when he was still with the MET.

A cold shiver ran through me at the thought that Brodie's name might be added to that list.

What was it that drove someone to murder after all this time?

Revenge, as Brodie said, seemed the most logical.

Blackwood had been ruined financially, through his own devices to be certain. An argument and duel that followed took the other man's life, though Blackwood had pleaded that he was acting in self-defense.

The man had lost everything, a dark reminder of my own father's dismal end.

What of Blackwood's family? What had happened to them? If they were still in London, would he go there?

What more might Mr. Dooley be able to tell me?

The weather had decided to remain miserable, wet, and cold.

I thought of Brodie. It was some comfort that he was to meet up with Munro. I was aware they were quite capable. The streets of London were familiar to both of them. Still, three men involved with that case years before were now dead...

Rather than return to Mayfair for clothing appropriate to the weather, I borrowed one of Brodie's jumpers and pulled it on over my undergarments. It carried a bit of the scent of cinnamon and made me feel somehow close to him.

Foolish, of course, yet it was perfect with my walking skirt for the weather. I appreciated the warmth on my neck— women's fashions could be quite lacking and not at all appropriate for trekking about London in the ice and mud.

I added my long coat, then gathered my travel bag with my notebook and umbrella.

The foul weather did not disappoint as I locked the office door and navigated the icy steps to the sidewalk by the street.

Mr. Cavendish emerged from the alcove that now also included a coal stove against the cold to warm himself, and

Rupert as well. There had been breakfast earlier from the Public House.

"Will you be needin' a driver, Miss Mikaela?" he inquired, which was his barely discreet way of inquiring where I was off to, after Brodie had no doubt spoken to him.

"New Scotland Yard on a matter that might be of assistance to the case."

He nodded, paddled out to the edge of the sidewalk and let out a shrill whistle over the usual noise on the street of coaches and cabs that paid no heed to the weather when a fare was to be earned.

A driver eventually arrived and eased his rig to a stop at the sidewalk. I gave the driver the destination, then climbed aboard.

Mr. Cavendish held the door open from the bottom of the gate.

"Up with you," he called to Rupert, who joined me with great excitement as well as mud.

"He gets a bit put out when the weather is like this and he hasn't been out and about."

"Following instructions, are you, Mr. Cavendish?" I inquired as he closed the door of the coach.

He grinned. "The ride will do him good."

The ride from the Strand to the embankment was not far; however, the weather had made a mess of things as usual during winter in London.

It was very near midday when we arrived. Rupert jumped down onto the walkway at the entrance. I paid the driver, and we entered the foyer of the New Scotland Yard.

Rupert frequently generates surprise when we are out and about. The young constable at the desk previously was quite taken aback and started to protest.

"We don't allow animals inside the premises, miss."

I rarely used my title, however...

"Lady Forsythe," I clarified. "And it's quite all right. He is with me. I would like to speak with Inspector Dooley if he is available, regarding an important matter."

Somewhat flustered by the situation, the young constable picked up the handpiece of the telephone and put through a call.

It was only a matter of minutes until Inspector Dooley arrived, an amused expression on his face as he assured the young constable that it was quite all right for the hound to be allowed inside the offices of the 'Yard.'

"You caused quite a stir, Miss Mikaela."

He escorted me into a private office. Rupert followed dutifully along.

I explained that Brodie had left earlier while I remained at the office to assist as I could.

He nodded. "Brodie spoke of it. And we have a good many men, plain-clothed, brought on extra duty to assist as well."

I explained the information I wanted that might be useful.

"What of Blackwood's family? If they remained in London, might he go there?"

He shook his head. "We already made inquiries. His wife and son left London shortly after the end of the trial, and all but disappeared. We were not able to find any indication they might have returned."

Convicted, sent to prison, his family destroyed by the scandal, and now Blackwood was taking his revenge.

"What hospital did he escape from? Have the people there been questioned?" I thought of the traces of morphine Brodie found on the chief inspector's shirt.

"What was he being treated for? It could be important."

"St. Bart's is the hospital. St. Bartholemew, that is. It's on my list for inquiries."

I thanked him and stood to leave.

"I'll accompany you, Miss Mikaela, though I doubt they'd allow that fine fellow inside," he added with a glance down at the hound. He was able to acquire a plain-clothed driver with the MET.

St. Bartholemew was the oldest hospital in London, located in West Smithfield very near St. Paul's Cathedral, an imposing grey stone building that filled an entire street block, the cathedral and graveyard nearby.

Prisoners, Mr. Dooley explained as we arrived at the main entrance, were taken there if there was an emergency or a prisoner became ill, which happened frequently. They were well guarded, treated for whatever illness, then returned to prison, though some did not as they did not survive.

What was the illness or emergency that brought Sir Edward Blackwood there? And what might it tell us?

I had worked previously with Mr. Dooley, as I had first known him, when Brodie was taken off in another direction on an inquiry case.

I was pleased for him when he made inspector, however he informed me that *'Mr. Dooley'* would do, as he was most familiar with that, the same as his wife called him, usually when she was in a temper.

He was congenial and likable, yet most proficient in his responsibilities, and a valuable resource for our inquiry cases.

He asked our driver to wait in the carriage park across from the hospital. Rupert remained there as well.

I waited in the room that had been set aside for visitors and families as Mr. Dooley made inquiries regarding the physician who had attended Blackwood when he was brought to hospital.

He eventually returned.

"The man we're to see is Dr. Metcalf. He was the physician on duty the morning Blackwood was brought in. The nurse will take us to his office."

It was located in the ward adjacent to the main hall, a substantial walk, then a climb to the second floor of the ward.

We waited in a small office until Dr. Metcalf joined us, a scholarly man with greying hair and that calm manner one would hope for in a physician. He greeted us, then took the chair behind a desk.

Mr. Dooley explained the reason we were there. Dr. Metcalf shook his head.

"A highly regrettable situation for a prisoner to escape. Has he been returned?"

"Not as yet," Mr. Dooley replied, after introducing me as a 'consultant' with the Metropolitan Police. "That is the reason we are here, in the hope that you might be able to provide information that could be useful."

"I will try, although there is very little I can tell you about the man. He was here briefly, examined and treated, then gone."

"Can you tell us the reason he was brought here?" I inquired.

"He had apparently been suffering for some time with symptoms that were quite severe and had grown worse, together with a constant fever. There was a concern it was something that could be contagious and might spread."

"What was it?"

"A cancer and quite advanced. Not contagious as first feared, but eventually fatal."

"Was he treated?" I inquired.

He nodded. "In such cases, the treatment is more for the comfort of the patient, if possible. We treated him for the pain. As for the fever, there is little that could be done. Pneumonia will eventually occur."

"And treatment for the pain?"

"The options are limited; however, he was given a strong measure of medicinal morphine. It can provide relief when carefully administered, as it can become habit-forming. Though, I suppose that is of little concern to the person who is dying from the disease."

It did explain the morphine stain Brodie had found on the chief inspector's clothes, apparently from the attack when he was murdered.

"How long might he live?" Mr. Dooley asked.

"That is unknown and depends very much on the patient. However, the cancer will progress, and the prisoner's condition was already substantially deteriorated. The treatment for pain is only a temporary solution. He would, however, undoubtedly seek out more of the drug, if possible, to control it."

He was thoughtful. "A very sad outcome in spite of the man's situation. The length of time he may have is unknown."

Unknown. Yet Blackwood had managed to carry out his revenge on those he believed had wronged him.

Mr. Dooley thanked the doctor for the information, and we returned to the carriage park where our driver waited, along with Rupert.

It was late in the day as Mr. Dooley escorted me back to the office.

"Not to worry," he assured me. "With the man's condition, alone on the street, with no money or persons he can rely upon, it is possible Blackwood is already dead."

I was well aware what he was attempting to do.

"You are not very good at it, you know."

"What is that?"

"Telling lies."

He winced as if he had been struck. "My dear wife has said the same. Still, I know Mr. Brodie. He is like a cat with nine lives, as the saying goes, also according to my Maeve."

Nine lives. I did wonder how many of those he had already used. And now, he faced a man who was dying and nothing more to lose, out for revenge?

Mr. Cavendish was there as Mr. Dooley's coach departed. He looked up at me from his platform as I didn't immediately go to the stairs.

I took out my notebook and pen.

"I need to send word to Mr. Brodie. It's important," I explained as I opened my notebook, and there in the shelter of the alcove, penned a brief note about what Mr. Dooley and I had learned.

A man desperate for morphine to dull the pain, and without resources, might not be difficult to find with assistance from someone like Mr. Brown, who was known to have certain 'enterprises' in such things.

The note was brief. I signed it with, *'Please be careful. M.B.'* and handed it to Mr. Cavendish.

He nodded. "I'll get it to the man who will get it to Mr. Brown. Not to worry, Miss Mikaela."

He tucked the note into his jacket.

I watched as he set off in the rain, a wake of icy water following him as he expertly traversed the Strand in spite of the flooded thoroughfare.

He was the second person in as many hours to remind me of that. Not that I was worried for Brodie.

He knew the streets and a good many people in them. I was confident that he would find Sir Blackwood, or perhaps his body.

It was undoubtedly a sin to hope for that, for those who believed in such things. I never had. As I climbed the stairs to the office, I preferred to believe in the lives of a cat.

I apologized to Rupert for that as I opened the door and stepped into the office.

It was cold inside, the fire in the stove having burned low after I left. But I had experienced that before.

The light from the electric cast shadows at the edge of the room. I had also experienced that several times before.

It was no different now, and yet it was because he wasn't there.

Bloody hell, I silently swore.

When had everything changed? Quite some time ago, that inner voice whispered, on the island off the coast of Greece when a dark-eyed man had refused to give in to my curses, threats, and excuses. A man who was there whether I wanted it or not...until I did. And a bloody Scot for all that.

There was nothing more to be accomplished here tonight. I could add what I'd learned today to my notes, yet I could do that at the townhouse. And my latest publishing endeavor was there, half finished, in the typewriter on my desk.

Mrs. Ryan would be there...

I wrote a note for Brodie, telling him that I was returning to Mayfair for the night, then looked down at a sound the hound made as he lay patiently at my feet, large eyes fixed on me, waiting.

"You are quite fond of Mrs. Ryan's suppers," I commented.

He immediately rose to his feet, head cocked, tail wagging.

"I thought as much," I replied to his obvious enthusiasm. I could almost see Brodie roll his eyes as I talked to Rupert.

"You will need to be particularly nice to Mrs. Ryan and mind your manners."

He was already waiting at the door as I laid the note on Brodie's desk where he would easily find it.

"Come along then," I told Rupert as I turned off the electric, closed the door, then set the lock.

At the street, I waved down a driver, no small task as more people sought the shelter of a cab or coach when the weather set in.

A familiar driver pulled his rig to the curb, water washing up onto the sidewalk from the wheels of the coach

"It's not a day to be out and about." Mr. Jarvis squinted out from under his billed cap through the downpour.

"I did attempt to arrange otherwise with the weather, however..." I replied, as I climbed aboard his coach. And Rupert was there as well. He grinned at me, as he settled himself on the floor of the coach.

Mr. Jarvis nodded. He was quite familiar with the hound's traveling about with me.

"Where will it be this fine end of day?"

"Mayfair," I replied.

"Number ten, Hanover Square it is then, Miss Mikaela," he replied and spoke to his team.

So much for any criticism about my conversations with Rupert, I thought, as the coach lurched away from the curb.

He watched from the darkened entrance of the tobacco shop beside the stairs to that office on the second-floor landing as the coach departed.

A surprise, he thought, having discovered the office of former inspector Angus Brodie. And an additional surprise in the scene he just witnessed—a woman.

Not the usual sort he would have expected of a former police inspector, now private inquiry agent, or the man who had tracked him through clubs and brothels and found him. But a lady by the way she spoke and her manner that he knew from his life...before.

It was gone now: his wife and son, his own father now dead these many years, friends or those he thought were friends.

They were all gone, including three of those who had taken it all from him. Now there was just one more, he thought, as the pain that he'd kept at bay reminded him of what the physician had told him at the hospital.

Time. It was slipping away as the pain tightened inside him. But there was still enough left to finish what he swore he would do.

He would take from Angus Brodie what the man had taken from him.

Mikaela, not a name heard often, but obviously someone important to Brodie. He had discovered that in that office on the second floor.

Slow, patient work on the lock, just the way a man in the next bunk over had showed him, a skill that would serve him well after he had served his sentence.

Thievery it was called, but time was against him with the cancer that grew inside him.

The disease that ate away at him was also the means for his freedom, brief though it might be. He would finish what he had vowed twelve years before as his sentence was handed down. She would help him do it. And then he would disappear for whatever time was left.

He gathered the coat tightly about him. He'd taken it from a table outside a seconds shop when he first left the hospital.

The knife in the waist of the pants, also taken from the seconds shop, would see it done.

The money in his pocket, taken from Chief Inspector Dawes, wasn't much—no doubt part of the man's retirement pension—but it was enough to finish this.

And then he would disappear for whatever time was left. Perhaps someplace warm, as the pain twisted like a knife.

He retrieved the vial of that sweet syrup from inside the coat, his only relief from the pain, temporary as it was.

He had wandered after escaping the hospital, hiding until he was able to find the clothes to replace his prison clothes.

That first night was spent in a vacant room in a crumbling tenement as far from the hospital as he could get. It was cold and miserable, but better than the prison block, where he had a pallet and blanket but nothing more.

In spite of his education and the position he'd once had in London society, he was not allowed in the "master's side" of Newgate, where the wealthy were housed. The ward where he had lived the past twelve years was crowded, damp, infested with lice and vermin, and disease-ridden.

No longer, he thought bitterly. No longer would he be forced to eat the never-ending daily ration of stale bread, gruel, and rotten potatoes. When the cancer set in, it was fish and milk, until that came back up and it was decided that he needed to go to the hospital.

It was his salvation, even as the physician grimly explained what was slowly killing him.

But there was still enough time to finish what he had begun, the one thing that had given him purpose in prison and the will to survive. And the means to carry it out was at Number Ten Hanover Square.

Thirteen

BRODIE ENTERED the boxing club in Bethnal Green by way of a back entrance.

"I'll stay here," Munro told him. "To make certain there are no surprise visitors while ye meet with Brown."

He nodded and took the stairs two at a time to the second floor.

The club was a place where lads with a week's wages in their pockets tried their fists against those who called themselves 'professional boxers,' fighting in the two raised rings surrounded by a houseful of those who came to watch and bet.

It smelled of cigarette smoke, sweat, and the drink that cost three times the price at a local tavern, amid shouts, cheers, and curses from those who gathered round.

Not so on the second floor, the noise and smells of the floor below left behind by the man who occupied the large office. He looked like a respectable businessman, as long as one disregarded the two guards at the door.

One of the guards nodded at Brodie and opened the door.

The man behind the large desk completed a meeting as he scooped bills and coin into a metal box.

A portion for the young woman who stood there was quickly scooped into a satin bag and tied off with satin cord.

"There's a girl," Mr. Brown commented. "A good night's work. Be certain to pay the other girls as agreed." Something in his voice changed, not quite threatening but a reminder.

"I'll not have 'em cryin' to my men that ye've been holding back their pay."

"I wouldn't cheat," she assured him. The truth in her claim went as far as the distance of the desktop.

"Ye would do well to remember what happened to Maisy when she decided to pay herself extra coin, instead of sharing it as agreed. You steal from the girls, yer stealin' from me."

"You have me word."

"There's a good girl, Lucy. I wouldn't want to have to send one of my men round to pay a visit."

Prostitution was just one of Mr. Brown's business enterprises that included extortion, protection offered businesses in the working-class area in that part of London, gambling, and drugs. Specifically, morphine brought into the country.

Brown was a man of many business interests that Brodie had once kept a watchful eye on when he was a constable with the MET.

Then, in his time as an inspector, he kept a distance from the illegal street trading, stolen goods in unregulated markets, and other activities that operated outside official regulations and taxes.

Unless it had to do with children, the poor who were sold for a few coins into lives of beggary, pan-handling, and prostitution. He had seen too much of that on the streets of Edinburgh as a child. Had even begged in order to survive, picked pockets, and seen what became of girls with no other trade except themselves.

Years before, he and Brown had struck a bargain of sorts. There was nothing in writing, only their word that they would keep to their own 'side of the street.'

There were occasional favors exchanged, but Brodie made it a rule to keep one ahead of Brown. It was a good way to stay alive. And somewhere through the years and favors, a grudging respect one for the other had grown. Although he had no doubt Brown could turn if there was enough profit. He made certain there never was.

Now? He'd received word to meet with the man, the result of the word he and Munro had put out on the streets through Brown's web of business associates, in doss houses, tenements, taverns, and pubs, searching for word of Blackwood.

Lucy, one of Brown's 'employees,' stopped as they met in the doorway, her expression clearly an offer.

"Get on with you," Brown told her. "That one's taken, by a lady no less, a real lady with red hair, a temper to match, and a particular skill with a revolver. I've met her and she's not one you would want to cross."

"Sorry," Lucy apologized with a pout, then left Brown's office.

"You would be the ruin of me, Brodie, if ye ever decided to take advantage. The lot of them wouldn't charge you a farthing to warm their beds."

"You sent word that ye'd received a message."

Brown nodded, opened the center drawer of the desk and took out a folded note.

"The cripple gave it to one of my men no more than an hour ago." He handed it across the desk.

Brodie read it, the elegant letters written by the lady with the red hair and that temper to match.

She had found information about Blackwood that might be useful. He was dying from a cancer and had been given morphine at the hospital for the pain before he escaped.

He would, no doubt, need more...

Do remember, church mice. M., she had signed it.

He smiled to himself as he folded the note and put it in his coat pocket. He looked up.

"The man is dying and in a great deal of pain, it seems. He likely has little or no funds, but he's in need of morphine."

Brown's sharp gaze narrowed. "I'll put the word out among my people." He gave Brodie a long look.

"When was the last time you slept?"

"A while ago," Brodie replied.

"There's a room at the next floor up."

"And find a blade between my ribs in the dark of night?" Brodie knew the man well.

Brown shook his head. "I cannot spare one of my men as I'm certain he would be the worst for an encounter with you. And take Munro with you. The man has a bad habit of leaving bodies about. It's bad for business. And no charge for the room," he added. "We will call it a 'favor' in exchange for your warning about the man needin' morphine. Ives, my man at the door, will see that ye have a cot and a blanket up at the room."

He shouted an order through the closed door and Ives appeared.

"Mr. Brodie and Mr. Munro will be our guests for the night. See them to their accommodation but take care. Mr. Brodie carries a firearm and Mr. Munro is particularly skilled with the blade."

MIKAELA

"You've hardly eaten," my housekeeper, Mrs. Ryan, scolded. "Hours it was, over a hot oven, and Mr. Brodie not about as well. It's a waste of good food."

I looked up. I would admit that I had little appetite, and I did appreciate Mrs. Ryan's thriftiness as well as care. Much like a mother, I supposed.

We did have that sort of relationship in addition to her being in my employ, a relationship strengthened after the death of her daughter Mary, who was a maid at Sussex Square, then for my sister Lenore.

Such a sad affair. It was her disappearance, along with my sister, that I had first encountered Brodie back in London.

He was referred to me by my great-aunt, of all persons, which did raise the question of why she might have needed the services of a private inquiry agent, which, after the years since, had yet to be explained.

'A man I could trust,' she had insisted and provided his address at the office on the Strand.

That recommendation was received with some skepticism at the time, as I did not have a particularly high regard for most men after certain childhood circumstances, and admittedly, such high esteem did seem a bit odd when I first encountered Mr. Cavendish, who occupied the alcove at the foot of the stairs outside the office. Along with the rather scantily dressed woman who emerged from that office.

I had considered the alternative, possibly acquiring the services of a gentleman by the name of Holmes, who was known to lend his services to clients in need. However, his reputation included a somewhat questionable use of narcotics, not to mention a habit of disappearing in the middle of an inquiry case.

I did have very definite requirements in that regard. In addition, I was determined to assist in the search for my sister, as I knew her habits, and Mary's as well, of course. I could be of assistance and needed someone who was amenable to that.

In spite of the odd man on his rolling platform who greeted me as I arrived, and the woman dressed in the chartreuse gown—'dressed' being a generous description—I kept my meeting with Brodie.

Which was the beginning of our working relationship, a somewhat unique friendship that I had never experienced.

I had once read a quote by Aristotle about friendship and thought it quite ridiculous at the time—that 'friendship was a slow ripening fruit.'

Yes, well, there was friendship, of course, and respect, which I had never experienced from a man.

There was that other thing that my great-aunt had spoken highly of...

I suppose I should have been warned at that first meeting by my own cautions when we met.

He was quite handsome, though informal with appearance —I remembered it well. With a workman's shirt open at the collar, his sleeves rolled back, cotton-spun trousers, and boots sorely in need of a polish, along with overlong hair that curled over his collar. All of it what a common worker might wear.

There was that dark gaze that fastened on me as I entered his office, his expression what could only be called...impatience. As if I had disturbed him at some important matter. And a bloody Scot of all things...

Oh, there was most definitely that other recommendation my great-aunt made.

That had come somewhat later. Friendship and then…a man I could trust who made my toes curl.

Together, somewhat reluctantly on his part, we had solved that first inquiry case. My sister was found safe. However, dear, sweet Mary was lost, brutally murdered.

I looked up at Mrs. Ryan who stood beside the table as she retrieved my plate with the now cold roast chicken she had labored over and an expression of disapproval on her face.

"I suppose I shall have to feed it to that flea-ridden beast," she announced, her Irish accent always somewhat stronger when she was in a temper.

"You do know that I adore you," I replied.

She made a sound that might mean anything. "And the supper was marvelous," I complimented her. "Mr. Brodie will be disappointed that he wasn't here to share it.

"You might put it in the icebox," I suggested. "With a portion for Rupert, of course."

Another sound. "A portion for the beast." She shook her head, much as a mother would have.

"Will you be taking coffee at your desk in the front parlor?" she asked.

It did seem that I had perhaps been forgiven. I smiled.

"Yes, please."

The fire in the fireplace was warm; the coffee was perfect with that hint of cinnamon that Mrs. Ryan insisted was good for me. And then there was a dram of Old Lodge, my great-aunt's whisky distilled in the Highlands, to smooth the edges of my nerves over the message I had given to Mr. Cavendish.

Was he able to find Brown's man who would get the message to Brodie?

Had he received it?

What of Blackwood?

Where was he now?

Was Brodie the next target?

I poured another dram of whisky and went to my writing desk.

I worked through the evening, adding notes to my notebook, then read back through the last chapter of my current Emma novel.

It was a thinly disguised account of an inquiry case I was involved in.

I smiled at the description of the rather handsome, strong-willed man who was now part of her adventures in murder. The last two novels had met with great success.

It did seem as if the ladies of London had a particular fondness for *'murder most foul,'* according to Sir William. Shakespeare, that is.

My good friend Templeton, who claimed to be connected to the spirit of Sir William, would be highly amused. She was presently on tour with her theater group. I did miss our often-bizarre conversations.

Mrs. Ryan had bid me goodnight some time earlier, not without a parting comment about supper.

"Shall I prepare supper tomorrow for one, miss?"

I hoped not. I did hope that Brodie would return, the business of Blackwood resolved. However...

"I will let you know. And once again, Mrs. Ryan, supper was magnificent," I complimented her.

"Not that anyone would know by the small amount you ate, not enough for a child. I put the roast chicken in the icebox and locked the door for the night," she continued. "Good night, miss."

And she was gone, mumbling something about her efforts with the sponge cake she had prepared for dessert.

I looked over at the hound stretched out across the rug before the fireplace.

"You do seem to have put on some weight," I commented. His response was the snoring that continued uninterrupted.

Then there was only the sound of the door closing from Mrs. Ryan's room beyond the kitchen, and the hiss of the fire in the fireplace as I continued the next chapter in Emma Fortescue's latest adventure.

It was well after midnight. Two paragraphs in more than two hours...!

I pulled the sheet of paper from the typewriter and wadded it in frustration. It joined several other pieces on the floor. I looked over at the hound.

I had obviously disturbed his sleep.

"What are you looking at, sir?" I demanded. Not that I expected an answer. I glanced at the clock on the mantel.

It was after midnight, several hours since supper...several more since I had sent that message to Brodie.

Was there some difficulty getting it to him? Had something happened to prevent Mr. Cavendish getting it to Brown's man?

Rupert groaned and laid his head back on the carpet.

It was quite marvelous, the way he was able to simply ignore everything around him and return to sleep. Not unlike someone I knew.

"Oh, bloody hell." There was nothing more to be done in the middle of the night.

In the morning, I would return to the office. Mr.

Cavendish would be there, and I would learn if he was successful in delivering the message.

I retrieved from my bag the revolver Brodie insisted that I carry, and put it into the pocket of my dressing gown, then went to the fireplace.

Rupert did not move a hair as I set the screen in front of the fireplace, one of those small things Brodie usually did when he was here. I then turned off the lamp on my desk, rechecked the lock on the front door, then turned off the electric in the hall and climbed the stairs to the second floor.

I placed the revolver on the floor beside the bed as Brodie did each night, then removed my dressing gown and crawled under the covers as the rain beat on the window.

There was a faint scratching at the door, then the familiar sound of Rupert's nails on the wood floor. He paused. Undoubtedly a question, if one was into communicating with animals.

Oh, very well, I thought. "Are you going to just sit there?"

He responded by leaping up onto the bed and settling himself without further ado at my feet. Undoubtedly a mistake on my part. It was Brodie's fault for not being there.

Where was Brodie? I thought, as the hound settled himself, quite content.

Had he received that message...? Was he safe?

In spite of my current bed partner, the bed seemed cold and empty. I tucked my feet against Rupert. At least my feet were warm...

It was some time later that a sound wakened me. Coming out of sleep, I realized that it was Rupert. He was no longer on the bed but somewhere near the door and obviously upset in a way that I recognized.

Another sound came then, far different, and seemed to come from downstairs.

I left the bed, put on my dressing gown, then retrieved the revolver from the floor beside the bed. I went to the door and slowly opened it, then placed a hand on the ruff at Rupert's neck that was standing up. He whined softly.

"Stay," I gave the command I had been teaching him. With mixed results, as he had a mind of his own.

He obeyed and stayed by my side as I left the room and went out onto the second-floor landing. Beside me, the hound growled, low and threatening, as I glanced about the ground floor, fully illuminated by a ceiling light in the foyer.

I was certain I had turned off the electric before I came upstairs. I listened for other sounds—the familiar clink of Old Lodge as Brodie poured a glass when he returned late at night, or the sound as he sat wearily in one of the chairs before the hearth.

I heard neither, as Rupert pulled against my hold on him.

It wasn't Brodie.

"Milady?"

Rupert whined softly as Mrs. Ryan called out from the entrance to the dining room next to the front hallway.

She was suddenly dragged into the light in the hallway, clad in her nightgown, the braid of her hair over one shoulder, a knife pressed against her throat by the man whose other arm was wrapped across her shoulders.

I raised the revolver as Rupert exploded with snarls and furious barking and would have charged down the stairs.

"Call off your hell hound and put the revolver down, or the old woman dies!"

For those few seconds, I glimpsed that strong Irish spirit on

Mrs. Ryan's face, fierce pride and grim determination as she shook her head. In spite of the man holding her with a knife at her throat, his eyes gleaming from pain and the morphine that pulsed through his veins.

I had no doubt that I had just met Sir Edward Blackwood.

Gone was the confusion when first coming out of sleep. I was now frightened and angry. Afraid for Mrs. Ryan, and furious at the despicable, drug-riddled man who held her.

I slowly descended the stairs with a death grip on Rupert. He struggled to break free, but I held on, certain that if he escaped it would mean Mrs. Ryan's death.

"Now, put down the weapon!" Blackwood rasped. "I will not hesitate to kill her."

I believed him and laid the revolver on the floor at the landing. No mean feat, as Rupert continued to whine and thrash.

"Step away," he ordered.

I stepped away from where I had laid it.

"Now put that beast in the dining room."

His voice was cold as ice, even as beads of sweat streamed down the side of his face, his features gaunt, eyes sunken with the disease that ravaged him and the narcotic that burned through him.

I dragged Rupert through the doorway of the dining room.

"Close the doors," Blackwood ordered, backing farther away.

I closed the sliding doors, Rupert barking furiously. I took a slow deep breath and forced myself to remain calm as I slowly turned around.

"What do you want?"

"What I have wanted the past twelve years...I want Inspector Angus Brodie," he whispered, his voice thin now, his face tightening as he sucked in a sudden breath, the pain there in his expression.

"I don't know what you're talking about." My thoughts raced as he continued to move toward the parlor with Mrs. Ryan his prisoner.

"I saw you." His voice was a ragged whisper as he stood with her in a pool of light that spilled from the entry hall into the parlor.

And then a forced smile, gruesome with the pain that twisted his features.

"You told the driver," he replied. "Number Ten Hanover Square."

He was there tonight! And not the first time, I thought, remembering that impression I'd had earlier, that I had seen someone watching the office.

It had been brief, and I thought I had imagined it...the office door unlocked though nothing taken.

He had been watching and waiting, even as he carried out those gruesome murders. Even with the effects of the morphine, it was obvious that he was intelligent. The drug only sharpened his anger, even as the words slurred and he struggled with them.

"Where is Angus Brodie?"

In the very least, he knew that we worked together, there was no point in arguing the matter. I attempted to bury my hand with the ring Brodie had given me in the folds of my dressing gown.

"He is obviously not here," I told him with disdain.

That sickening slow smile.

"Do you know where he is?" he demanded again.

"I have no idea." It was not a lie.

Brodie was out there somewhere, searching for Blackwood.

He might be anywhere. That drugged gaze narrowed. He reached out and seized me by the wrist, dragging my hand from the folds of fabric where it had been hidden. He stared at the ring on my finger.

"You are his wife!" he announced with something very near childish glee. "How very perfect. So much more than I could have hoped for."

I jerked my arm away from him.

What was he talking about? Was he delirious from pain and the morphine?

He grabbed Mrs. Ryan and shoved her toward me. He aimed the revolver at her.

"You will dress warmly, then immediately return. You are going to deliver a message for me, and you will get rid of that cursed animal! Now! And if you do not return, I will kill her." He aimed the revolver at me.

Mrs. Ryan looked at me, her expression pale. I nodded for her to do as he said, and she quickly left through the dining room, closing the doors behind her against any possible escape by Rupert.

His furious barking abruptly lessened, then ceased altogether. I could only assume that she had sent him outside.

She eventually reappeared, dressed 'warmly' as ordered, in one of her usual gowns, sturdy walking boots, with a coat over. The braid still hung over her shoulder. She had not taken the time to put her hair up as she usually wore it.

"What is the message?" she asked in a voice that steadily grew stronger. "How am I to get it to him when I don't know where he is?"

"You are to take it to the cripple who occupies the alcove at the Strand. I believe you know what I'm speaking of?"

She nodded. "I know of it. What is the message he is to carry?"

"Tell Angus Brodie that I will take from him what he took from me. You're to tell him exactly that. Brodie will know the meaning of it. Do you understand?"

She nodded. "I do," she replied, then with a look at me, left, slamming the door behind her.

It was a pointless gesture. Still, I admired her spirit as I watched through the leaded glass in the door when she left, with Rupert at her heel, to deliver that message for Brodie to Mr. Cavendish.

Blackwood would take from Brodie what Brodie had taken from him?

I could only guess what that might mean, and it seemed that I was now part of it.

"You will dress as well," Blackwood said after she had gone.

He started toward me, the revolver aimed directly at me. He motioned me toward the stairs and followed.

My thoughts raced for some advantage. I was at a disadvantage as long as he had the revolver. I thought then of the blade I usually carried in my boot, given to me by Munro.

"Ye never know when ye might need it," he said at the time.

Yet a knife was no match for a firearm, and it was obvious that Blackwood was clearly unstable due to the pain of the cancer or the effects of the morphine, perhaps both. Still, I needed to wait for an opportunity where I might be able to stop whatever madness he was determined to carry out.

I could hope that Mrs. Ryan would promptly deliver that message, but then Mr. Cavendish would need to get it to Brodie. There was no way to know how long that might take. My only weapon at present was my refusal to be intimidated and to wait for an opportunity to escape.

"I do not have any weapons in my rooms, and I am perfectly capable of dressing myself," I informed him at the stairs.

"No doubt, yet I prefer not to take the chance that you might escape. You see, you are part of this, Lady Forsythe."

I was past any possibility of intimidation. I was furious. Yet, it would do no good at the moment.

I was grateful that I had left on my chemise and petticoat.

When I reached the door of my bedchamber, I quickly stepped inside, pushed the door closed and dressed before the door opened. I finished tying the laces on my boots, then grabbed my jacket.

There was only one man I dressed, or undressed, for!

When we returned downstairs, Blackwood instructed me to call for a driver.

And we waited.

"What are you going to do?"

A slow smile. "I am going to pay Mr. Brodie back for what he has done to me."

I had not known Brodie then, and he had never spoken about the cases he pursued as an inspector with the MET.

Yet, from the few things I knew from him about Blackwood, the circumstances far too closely mirrored the circumstances that led to my own father taking his life. Three people who were directly involved in his imprisonment were now dead. I could only assume that he intended to kill Brodie as well.

"I understand."

He smiled that faint, drugged smile filled with pain.

"You cannot possibly understand what it is to lose your family, your home, everything."

But I did, far too well.

The driver arrived and Blackwood motioned for me to go ahead of him. He held back briefly.

I ran to the driver then, but Blackwood quickly caught up, a hand on my arm.

He pushed me up into the coach then closed the door, the revolver in his pocket pointed at me as he gave the driver instructions.

Fourteen

THE BOXING CLUB, BETHNAL GREEN

BRODIE

HE WAS awake in an instant with a sense that someone had entered the room— someone who hadn't been invited. He reached for the revolver when a sound came that might have been surprise as he found the matches and struck one.

The flame caught, momentarily casting light across features as the man who had made that sound tried to fight off the other one, who pinned him against the wall beside the door— Munro.

Brodie lit the nearby lantern. It sputtered to life, growing stronger as it found the oil in the bowl of the lantern, the man Munro had caught dangling like a fatted pig—Ives.

"There's been word," Ives managed to choke out as Brodie came to his feet and crossed the room.

"What word?" Brodie demanded.

"It came from Mr. Brown's man," Ives managed to squeeze out a reply. "Ease off, I'm just delivering the message."

"By stealing into the room," Brodie demanded.

"He said to bring you. Best speak with him."

"It would be easy to gut him like a fish," Munro commented.

"And wot of the dozen or so others who are no doubt about the place?" Brodie commented with a bit of dark humor. "A few more than we might prefer. Let us see what Mr. Brown has learned."

Ives cursed as Munro finally released him. "If I had me way..."

"If you had yer way, you would be dead," Munro told him.

They followed Ives down to the second floor where Brown sat at his desk, the sky pale with first light through a window beyond.

Had Brown received word where Blackwood could be found?

"Your man, the one who goes about on that platform like the devil was chasing him. He sent word that you need to get back to the Strand straight away."

"What's happened?"

"He didn't tell my man the purpose, only threatened to take his legs out if he failed to get word to you."

Mr. Cavendish had spent twenty years at sea until an accident aboard ship took his legs and left him land-bound. But, if need be, he could be quite dangerous, and had been known to use the deception of his infirmity to catch others unaware.

He was quick and strong, in great part due to the physical demands of his own personal transportation. He had seen the man take another man three times his size off his feet at the knees. The rest of the lesson was administered with the knife he carried but was rarely forced to use for such encounters.

Mikaela was fond of the man and always called him *Mr.* Cavendish, a sign of respect. Now, with the need to find Blackwood, if Mr. Cavendish said that the matter was urgent, it was urgent.

"I thank you, Mr. Brown." Brodie then nodded to Munro and left the boxing house as the first participants arrived for a morning bout.

"We'll be seein' each other, my friend," Brown called after them as they left the boxing club, found a driver, and promised twice the fare as they left Bethnal Green.

Brodie cursed the weather and the traffic on the street, even at that early hour of the morning. Still, they arrived at the Strand in quick time, Mr. Cavendish rolling out from the alcove as the driver pulled to the curb. He had the driver wait.

"I used the key Miss Mikaela gave me and put a woman upstairs," Mr. Cavendish informed him. "Mrs. Ryan... She brought word from Mayfair."

~

#204 THE STRAND

Brodie quickly took the stairs with Munro a short distance behind. He threw open the door to the office.

Mrs. Ryan rose from the chair across from his desk.

"Saints be praised, you're here Mr. Brodie!"

"What's happened? Tell me!"

He listened to all of it—Blackwood's threats reaching back across the years, what'd he'd lost—his family, his home, the family fortune. Threats that were made when Brodie, with the help of others, finally tracked him down.

Then the murder charge against Blackwood, the trial that followed. He'd avoided the hangman's noose and was sentenced to Newgate.

Never once did he show the least remorse for the life he'd taken, claiming he was innocent and had been wronged, protests and bold threats he made from the dock at the Old Bailey.

After the trial, articles filled the crime sheet of the Times. Even then, Blackwood refused to claim responsibility for the mistakes he'd made or the man he'd killed.

Instead, he blamed those who caught him—for tracking him down that last day, and for the loss of everything, the mistress he kept, the club he belonged to, the loss of his home and family fortune, the divorce that followed, and the loss of his son, as his wife took the child and fled the scandal.

He swore revenge.

Mrs. Ryan hesitated.

"Tell me all of it," Brodie told her.

"He said that he would take from you, what you have taken from him. Oh, Mr. Brodie... Miss Mikaela is strong, but I'm afraid for her!"

"Aye." He comforted her as best he could.

"What do ye want to do?" Munro asked from where he stood at the open doorway. He had heard the message given to the woman to deliver.

"I need to go to Mayfair," Brodie replied, a familiar coldness tightening inside him.

That message—that Blackwood would take from him what he had taken from the man—was even grimmer with drugs and the cancer feeding the insanity.

Such viciousness was no stranger to Brodie. He had encountered it before on the streets, driven by hunger, poverty, and desperation. But he had closed the door on that life, on people like Blackwood, for which there was only depravity and revenge. Blackwood had thrown the door open.

What would he find when he got to Mayfair?

Munro saw the grim expression on the face of the man who was like a brother.

Nothing was said as Brodie pushed past him and then strode down the stairs in the pouring rain to the street below. It wasn't necessary.

There were too many years between them, too many cold nights shared in a rat-infested hideaway trying to survive, a loaf of bread stolen and shared, a bond that went beyond blood.

Mr. Cavendish was there at the bottom of the stairs, with the hound beside him. He nodded and whistled sharply for a driver.

He greeted the man who swung his rig about and pulled to the curb. Brodie climbed inside before the coach came to a full stop.

"Take the hound with you," Mr. Cavendish said, not a question, as Munro swung up into the coach.

"Get on with you now," he told Rupert, and the hound quickly followed.

Brodie shouted their destination. Mr. Jarvis swung the team about and sent waves of water exploding beneath the wheels from the driving rain.

Brodie saw the smoke before they reached Hanover Place. Then the fire at the townhouse, the street before it filled with the wagons and water tenders of the fire brigade.

"I will take from you what you have taken from me!" A desperate last threat as Blackwood screamed from the dock at the court.

That knot inside Brodie tightened into a hard, cold fist as he vaulted out of the coach and ran toward that fire.

He threw off the hand on his arm as he reached the steps.

"She's not there!" Munro shouted over the roar of the fire

and the explosion of water from a pumper truck as Brodie pulled him back.

"She was taken away by the man the housekeeper spoke of!"

A crewman from the fire brigade was there, his face smudged from the smoke as he shouted.

"A gentleman across the way informed us when we arrived. He saw a coach leave just as the fire began. Sorry, sir," he apologized, as he no doubt assumed it was his residence.

Not his, but near enough in the time they had been together there, Brodie thought.

"The best we can hope for now, sir, is to prevent it spreading to the other residences," he said in parting as he ran and rejoined his men as the fire engulfed the townhouse.

'I will take from you…'

Beside them, the hound whined pitifully, as Brodie stared at the flames. He suddenly turned and ran back to the coach.

"I know where Blackwood has taken her."

When he reached the coach, he shouted up to Mr. Jarvis.

"Victoria Station! And hurry!"

MIKAELA, VICTORIA STATION

He was mad, I was certain of it, as he pushed me ahead of him through the crowd of arriving and departing passengers. His hand tightly clasped my arm, the revolver in his other hand concealed in the pocket of his coat, its barrel pressed against my back.

I couldn't help but think about that message he'd given Mrs. Ryan to deliver to Brodie.

Had she reached the office? Even if she had, would Mr. Cavendish be able to find him to deliver that message? What did it mean?

'I will take from you what you've taken from me.'

His freedom, lost twelve years before, when Brodie was an inspector with the MET and had been given the case to find Blackwood after that duel that had taken the other man's life?

Or was there more to his deranged plan, and I was now the helpless lure in his trap for Brodie?

What part did Victoria Rail Station have to play in this? Did he hope to escape, perhaps taking me with him? Where?

Dover seemed the most likely, since the Victoria line connected there, and then take a ferry across the channel? To what? Freedom?

What was there for him now, after all this time?

Ever since leaving the townhouse, I went through everything I had learned from Burke at the Times from the articles he had written about Blackwood. Columns written at the time of the murder in the aftermath of that duel, and the trial that had followed.

Blackwood had lost everything according to Burke's account—his family home, his position in society, his wife and child when they fled the scandal, what was left of his life to be spent in Newgate prison, a place as good as death, some said.

I thought again of that message he'd given Mrs. Ryan: *'I will take from you what you have taken from me.'*

He had to be deranged, perhaps insane, considering all that had happened since his escape, but what he intended was clear...to take from Brodie what had been taken from him.

Did that included killing him, since Blackwood was now dying of cancer, the morphine only delaying it long enough to come here...?

If he received that message, Brodie would come after me. I was certain of it as I scanned the faces among those we passed.

And he would die.

I continued to watch the faces of the passengers who departed the train that had arrived at the platform, people at the ticket counter we passed, and those around us as we moved along the platform to the next train that waited.

Was Brodie already there, somewhere amidst those who chatted amongst themselves, some not even passengers, perhaps escaping the weather and usual gloom of London in winter?

Would he be able to find us? There were at least a dozen platforms and an equal number of booking offices with the names of the rail companies serviced by the rail station.

The answer was there as Blackwood jerked painfully at my arm and pulled me from the crowd before the booking offices for the Dover line.

"Here!" he said, a sharp sound as he winced with pain. "We will wait here!"

I thought of alerting the clerk at the ticket counter as he assisted an elderly man and woman with their tickets, but decided against it. I would not endanger anyone in Blackwood's mad scheme.

I glanced about for any sign of Brodie. It was possible he never received that message.

It was obvious that Blackwood was suffering. I felt no sympathy. The man was a murderer, and he was dying.

What would he do if Brodie failed to appear? How long was Blackwood willing to wait?

The answer was there in that message.

He would wait here, or some other place known to both of them, and then take what had been taken from him.

The crowd that moved about us began to thin as passengers boarded their train. While others entered a nearby shop or one of the refreshment rooms that served tea and meals while they awaited their own departures.

Might there be a means of escape at one of the shops, I thought, as I felt once more the weakness in the hand that gripped my arm.

Blackwood was weak, however, not dead. He had sensed my movement, and his hand tightened, immediately alert once more.

"Not yet, Lady Forsythe!" he snarled. "But soon enough. I want Detective Brodie to feel what I felt when I lost my family. I want him to watch you die! And then it will be his turn!"

Detective Brodie? He *was* mad.

I saw it in Blackwood's eyes and heard it in his voice. Anything I attempted needed to be done quickly. That revolver at my back was a reminder. I would not endanger others.

The next train rolled into the station at the far end of the track. A rail clerk walked past and announced the arrival of the Dover-bound train. Those who had waited in one of those refreshment rooms began to fill the platform once more.

It was distant at first among the conversations that around us, amid the clatter and hiss of the train as it rolled toward us.

Then nearer, amidst sudden shrieks and shouted warnings from waiting passengers...

Fifteen

I WAS THROWN BACK against the wall of the shop where we had been standing, suddenly joined by a snarling, familiar blur of white and brown fur.

Rupert? It had to mean that Brodie was near!

It was the moment I had hoped for, as Blackwood scrambled to regain his footing and I was momentarily free of that death grip.

His raised his hand with the revolver.

Three men were dead, and Brodie was supposed to be next.

In that moment I experienced an emotion I had felt only once before, when I believed that I had lost my sister. A coldness that trapped the air in my lungs—anger! For Blackwood and what he was determined to carry out in his insane plot for revenge!

His gaze met mine as he tried to fight off Rupert. He was too close for me to sweep his legs out from under him. His enraged gaze met mine, and I struck, driving my elbow into his face.

He howled in pain, shocked as blood spurted from his nose. He cursed and came at me.

I heard my name as Brodie pushed through the crowd of stunned passengers, then saw him raise his arm, the revolver in his hand. Then I saw the conflicted expression on his face at the risk of firing amid the crowd of screaming and running passengers.

Rupert continued to attack as I scrambled to retrieve the revolver Blackwood had dropped. I heard a dreadful sound and then a familiar whine as I reached it and turned back around.

Blackwood stood over Rupert, a bloodied knife in his hand. At his feet, Rupert whined again and fought to get to his feet, then lay still.

Blackwood cursed, eyes glazed with pain, morphine. And the certainty of his own death?

He laughed, a cruel broken sound of madness as he stumbled away. When I would have gone after him, I was stopped by a strong grip on my arm.

"Ye canna risk it," Brodie said.

He followed, cutting through the throng of passengers, past a baggage trolley and the startled porter.

Munro appeared with two constables. He glanced briefly over at me, then followed. I ran after them.

Blackwood glanced back, the expression on his sunken features a terrifying mask as he stumbled, caught his balance, then suddenly stopped. I couldn't hear the drug-filled words he shouted over the terrified screams of the passengers. It wasn't necessary.

As Brodie closed in, Blackwood staggered from the effects of pain and the morphine, then launched himself toward the rail car of the train stopped at the platform.

Brodie shouted as he ran after him, whether in a last effort to stop Blackwood or warn him was uncertain. Then he suddenly halted along with Munro and the two constables.

Instead of attempting to enter the rail car, Blackwood climbed over the space between the two cars, fell, scrambled back to his feet and ran toward the adjacent tracks—directly into the path of a departing train as it gathered speed.

There was the sudden jarring sound, a rumble and clatter, and the screech of wheels on the metal rails, too late as the engineer attempted to stop the train.

Blackwood was thrown between the two rail tracks, his body bloodied and mangled.

I turned away. I had seen dead bodies before, but his was especially gruesome. Yet, somehow a just and fitting end for a man determined to carry out his scheme of revenge.

I glanced back down the platform where passengers slowly carried on. Some continued to gather as Mr. Dooley and two constables made their way across the tracks to the body. Others moved around the area where I had fought Blackwood, and where Rupert lay.

I ran back to Rupert and fell to my knees. He was still alive as I gently stroked his head, but his breathing was shallow. He gave a faint thump of his tail as I held him and spoke to him, and promised him Mrs. Ryan's sponge cake if he would stay.

"Might this help, miss?" a rail attendant asked as he stood beside us. He handed me a towel. "For the wound."

I nodded and took the towel. I pressed it against the wound on Rupert's side.

And then Brodie was there. He crouched down beside me.

"Are ye all right, lass?" he gently asked.

I looked up. Tears streamed down my face. And I never cried!

"Oh, Brodie..." I wept.

It was ridiculous, of course. How many times had Brodie cursed Rupert—as worthless, troublesome, a beggar and thief.

Most of it was true. But worthless?

Not when he made me laugh over his penchant for Mrs. Ryan's sponge cake or biscuits from the Public House. Almost, but not quite, with the things he scavenged from the streets and brought back with him like a trophy he'd found. Most certainly not when he attacked Blackwood.

Brodie took off his jacket and wrapped it around him.

I sat on the floor of coach and held him, wrapped in Brodie's jacket. He made not a sound and barely stirred as we sped across London to Holborn.

When we arrived, Brodie carried him into the back of Mr. Brimley's shop.

"I've not treated an animal before," the chemist said with a look over at me in the back of his shop. He smiled gently.

"But there is always a first time. The ancient Egyptians were quite skilled in such things, you know. Animals were important to them."

"He's in good hands, lass," Brodie assured me. "If anyone can save him, Mr. Brimley would be the one."

I knew he was right, yet leaving was difficult. I stroked Rupert's head.

"You have to get well. What am I to do with all the sponge cake?"

He licked my hand as he always did, as if to reassure me. Ridiculous as that seemed.

Brodie's hand closed around mine as we left the shop, with Rupert in Mr. Brimley's care. I would have trusted no one else.

Mr. Jarvis nodded from atop the coach where he had waited. I glanced down at my skirt, stained with blood.

"I should return to the townhouse for other clothes." I caught the look on Brodie's face.

"The office might be best," he suggested, something in his voice.

"I have nothing there except my long coat. I need to go to the townhouse."

It was undoubtedly something he didn't understand, the need to remove those blood-stained clothes, a reminder of what had happened today.

Or was it something else, by the way that dark gaze softened?

"I'll go with ye."

It seemed that Blackwood had not failed entirely as we arrived in Mayfair and Mr. Jarvis turned down the coach path at Hanover Place as rain began to fall.

I caught sight of the chimney, then the blackened walls that were all that remained of the townhouse as Mr. Jarvis pulled the team to a stop and I stepped down.

"The fire brigade did what they could," Brodie gently explained. "The gentleman across the way saw Blackwood set the fire before he left with ye."

I thought of that message Blackwood had sent for Brodie —*'I will take what you have taken from me.'*—his family home, his reputation, his wife and son gone.

He had most certainly been partly successful as I walked up the blackened stone steps and stood at what had once been the entrance to the townhouse.

I glanced across the way to the residence of the gentleman who had seen it all, then to my neighbor directly next. The wall nearest to her townhouse appeared unharmed except for a bit of soot from the fire and water from the fire brigade's efforts.

"Was anyone harmed?"

"The man with the brigade assured me no."

I nodded. That was, of course, most important.

I peered through the still smoldering rubble of what had once been my sanctuary. Where I had planned my travel adventures and wrote my first novel, along with the ones that followed, purchased with the royalties from that first book. It had become Brodie's home as well. Gone. All of it gone.

For a man who had nothing most of his life, it must seem preposterous to mourn the loss. Yet, I heard that quiet understanding that was always there in the softness of my name as he took me into his arms and brushed a tear from my cheek.

"It is only stone and brick," I said, my head on his shoulder, his hand gentle as he stroked my hair—the only thing that really mattered. "The office will do nicely."

Mr. Cavendish was there as we arrived. He glanced expectantly about, and I knew the reason. I explained what had happened.

He nodded, his mouth working with some emotion as I told him the hound had been injured. For a man who could be quite fierce in some matters, stoic in others, he was taken aback.

"I'd best look in on him then. He'll not take to bein' away from the alcove, or you, miss, for that matter."

I watched as he set off through the misty rain, a man who was strong enough to endure the handicap that had become his life, even feared by some he encountered, yet undone by the thought that Rupert had been injured and needed him.

Sixteen

SIX WEEKS LATER

MORE EASILY SAID THAN DONE, we discovered, as we established full-time residence at the Strand.

Improvements had previously been made with the newly installed water closet and the lift, which was promptly repaired.

However, while it had once been adequate for Brodie in the past and both of us when a case required, it was a great deal smaller than the townhouse, and we often found ourselves stepping over each other as we went about the days and weeks that followed the Blackwood case.

I had noticed that my clattering away at my typing machine was bothersome as I wrote the last of our case notes, then went on to my next Emma Fortescue novel, delayed after the fire at the townhouse. And then there was the matter of the new clothes I was forced to purchase.

Brodie and I had previously shared a cabinet with his shirts and trousers and the few things I kept there. It proved some-what challenging when he emerged one morning as he dressed for a meeting with the Home Secretary after the conclusion of the Blackwood case, dangling one of my silk undergarments that he'd found in the drawer with his wool jumpers.

"Ye know that I prefer ye without yer underthings..." he said, dangling a silk chemise. The threat was subtle, but there nonetheless.

Still, there were moments when we were stepping over each other.

My sister Lenore and her husband James suggested that we might take up the extra room at their residence. I caught the look on Brodie's face when I mentioned their offer.

"With young Miss Catherine crawling about, causing the usual chaos?" he replied.

I had to admit that, as much as I adored my niece, I was in agreement on that. We made a polite excuse when Linnie unexpectedly discovered she was to have another child.

James was delighted. My sister was somewhat taken aback by the possibility of two babies barely more than a year apart. I graciously declined the offer, and I believe they were greatly relieved.

"You might consider taking up your old room here at Sussex Square," Aunt Antonia suggested one morning when I needed to leave the office.

Brodie had set off earlier to meet with a new client who had been referred to us by Mr. Holmes, who was taking himself off to India.

They did seem to get along quite well no doubt due to their common profession with private inquiries. I personally thought the man quite odd, and there were rumors of his strange habits. Yet he was quite proficient in the ancient art of self-defense and complimented me after we encountered one another at the gymnasium.

"Remarkable," he said at the time. "A woman with the ability to protect herself. Mr. Brodie is a brave man."

I had assured him that 'Mr. Brodie' was well aware of the training I had acquired while on one of my extended travels.

And then there were engaging conversations with Mr. Holmes over supper at one of his favorite restaurants when I accompanied Brodie. One of those conversations included the necessary use of a firearm from time to time with the nature of the inquiry business.

Rather than asking to be excused from the conversation I had listened attentively as they discussed the advantages and disadvantages of certain firearms.

Brodie usually carried the revolver he had become most familiar with in his time as an inspector with the MET. He had provided me with one imported from the United States after my friend Templeton returned with one.

"It's not the model most of the men carry in parts of the country," Templeton had claimed, "however it is very handy if a man...shall we say, *takes liberties*."

She was somewhat notorious for her affairs, including one with Munro that lasted for some time.

The weapon fit quite well into my travel bag as well as the pocket of my walking skirts.

"I will warn ye that she is most proficient with it," Brodie had cautioned Mr. Holmes.

"A woman with a revolver? A dangerous but exciting possibility," Mr. Holmes commented at the time.

In the aftermath of the end of the Blackwood case, Brodie and I attended the funerals of those who had been his victims.

It was sad and a reminder of the seriousness of the inquiry business, that not all cases were resolved as easily as Lady Ambersley missing necklace, the only victim poor dear Bitsy, which I learned was banished to the solar by Lord Ambersley, rather than have access to the entire manor.

As for Blackwood, he was an escaped prisoner at the time of his death. His body was returned to Newgate, then buried within the prison grounds, we read in an exclusive notice on the crime sheet written afterward by Mr. Burke. Blackwood's resting place, under the flagstones of the passage known as Dead Man's Walk.

Quite dramatic that, I thought. But that was Theodolphus Burke, and I had promised that he would have the exclusive details from that last encounter at Victoria Station.

Rupert had recovered due to Mr. Brimley's care, skill learned at university where he studied to be a physician. Not altogether different than working on a severed foot or hand that occupied the jars in the back room of his shop.

When Rupert finally returned to the Strand, he was well groomed except for a long scar across his side, where Mr. Brimley had been forced to remove his mangy coat in order to operate and sew him back together.

There was a full sponge cake waiting for him as a gift from Mrs. Ryan, who had moved back to Sussex Square. Temporarily, she informed us, only until Brodie and I found a suitable residence.

Aunt Antonia expressed the hope that it would be sooner rather than later, as Mrs. Ryan had taken over the kitchen at Sussex Square, much to the dislike of her own cook, who threatened to quit.

"I was forced to increase the woman's wage to prevent her leaving," she told me over a dram of Old Lodge whisky one afternoon when I called on her and Lily, a visit which had become part of my routine when Brodie seemed to become testy over some matter.

My policy in such situations? Best to not be there, I discovered. And truth be told, afterward was far more...interesting.

As for our search for a new residence? It was always possible to take one of the smaller residences at Sussex Square. Munro had moved into the one nearer the stables when it was decided that a room near the servants' quarters was not appropriate.

I wasn't certain what that meant, but I thought it might have to do with a particular maid in my great-aunt's service.

I did not want to know and did not ask after Munro's somewhat colorful relationship with my friend Templeton.

There had been that vivid mural discovered in her country home as Brodie and I pursued a previous inquiry case. While I considered myself to be an enlightened woman, that mural had been most...colorful. I would leave it at that if anyone asked. Brodie had merely smiled at the time.

As I spent more time at Sussex Square in the weeks following the conclusion of the Blackwood case, I did notice what my great-aunt had spoken of regarding Lily.

She did seem preoccupied with some matter. I often found her in the sword room practicing with the rapier. Or out at the stables where the report of a firearm could be heard. Recently I had seen her at the writing desk in her room where she had finished something she was working on—a thank-you note, she said at the time.

We shared company often, and I did appreciate the time spent together, much like a sister, or 'daughter' as Brodie pointed out.

"Ye are getting on a bit, lass. And she is more the young lady now."

Getting on? I did not consider the age of thirty years to be 'getting on,' particularly since my great-aunt was a very young and spry eighty-seven. Although I might be tempted to adopt her response whenever the subject of her age came up.

She simply told whoever was bold enough to ask that she was not a day over fifty years of age.

"It doesn't matter what they think," she had announced. "Only what I believe."

A most fascinating response for someone who had a Viking longboat out on the green awaiting the day when it would be needed to send her off in a blaze of glory...if she should need it once she reached a ripe old age.

The issue of where we were to live until we found suitable residence continued to linger out there unresolved.

I had briefly viewed properties that were available, yet they were either rat-filled tenements at the edge of the Strand or an overdone residence at the edge of Mayfair.

It was Aunt Antonia who suggested that I simply have the townhouse rebuilt in Mayfair.

"After all, dear, you own the ground where the townhouse once was, and the other people in Mayfair would assuredly appreciate it for their own property values."

So, after discussion with Brodie, to which he replied, "It can be whatever you choose, but be finished with it. We have three new inquiry cases, and one is with the Home Secretary."

It was decided, and I spoke with my great-aunt regarding a recommendation as to who should build it.

"That might be difficult, dear. The last construction was the manor at Sussex Square. Thomas Matthews was the contractor...however, that was well over a hundred years ago. I'm certain he must be dead."

Of course.

"His grandson might be able to assist. He did the installation of the lift. His father, that would be Thomas's son, took care of the electric. I highly recommend their work."

I contacted young Alan Thomas and made arrangements to meet him and his father at the site where the townhouse had been before the fire. His father remembered working on Sussex Square.

"How does her ladyship like the lift?"

I answered that carefully so as not to offend the man. Neither he nor his son had been available for the installation of the lift at the office.

"It is a marvelous thing, however a work in progress," I tactfully replied.

He roared with laughter. "She is a rare one, that. Told me a story about an ancestor who was a highwayman. Not that I believed her. No offense, Lady Forsythe, but the older ones pull yer leg once in a while."

Pull the leg. I would like to see that one. I did not argue the point.

It did seem, however, that we were in for a lengthy rebuilding process. Mr. Matthews warned it might be a year or more, depending on his ability to get the appropriate materials.

I decided not to tell Brodie until later. It was always best to pick my moments or leave a note on the chalkboard. He was just beginning our inquiry case on behalf of the Home Secretary, which held the potential to be very difficult considering the well-placed people it might involve.

I returned from my initial meeting with Mr. Matthews over the proposed construction of the townhouse once the rubble had been cleared away. With the spring season very near, he hoped to make progress.

I entered the office and suddenly stopped as two rather grim expressions greeted me from Brodie and Munro.

Rupert, with his shaved coat mostly grown back except for the scar, had accompanied me from the street.

"What is it?" I inquired.

They both appeared quite serious, and I braced myself for some word regarding my great-aunt or possibly some other catastrophe from Sussex Square. Perhaps Mrs. Ryan threatening staff with a cleaver—there had been that one episode after she returned to Sussex Square following the fire. Or possibly Mrs. McAbernathy, my great-aunt's housekeeper, threatening to depart over some disagreement.

I caught the look that passed between them.

"Miss Lily has left Sussex Square," Munro replied.

"Left...?" I looked from one to the other. "What do you mean? Left? Where has she gone?"

"Sir Laughton called on Lady Montgomery this mornin'."

Sir Laughton, my aunt's lawyer. What did he have to do with this?

I immediately found a driver.

That question and more were all the more urgent as I arrived at Sussex Square and found Sir Laughton with my great-aunt in the salon.

"Munro is at the office. He said that Lily is gone?"

Sir Laughton rose from the chair beside the table before the hearth. "She asked me to give you this, but not until afterward. She is also my client, and as she is of legal age as far as we know, I was required to honor her wishes."

Afterward? What did that mean? I tore open the envelope.

Dear Mikaela,

I have received word from Dora, my good friend from the 'Church,' to whom I owe my life from before. She is in some

*difficulty and frightened, and it is necessary for me to return to
Edinburgh.
I have learned a great many things from you and
Mr. Brodie, and know you would not hesitate to help
someone in need.*

*Thank you.
Lily*

It might have been written by any well-educated, proper young lady.

I looked over at my great-aunt.

"She has returned to Edinburgh. What difficulty? Did she say anything to you?"

"No dear, not that I am surprised. You did not notify me before taking yourself off to Crete on your Greek travels."

"That is not the same at all," I replied. "How will she get on when she arrives? Where will she stay? She has no means..."

"Not precisely true," Sir Laughton replied. "I have to admit that I have concerns from her prior experience in Edinburgh, as a lady's maid in a house of prostitution. However, she is quite resourceful," he continued.

"She gave me this and asked if I would hold it against a loan of funds."

It was a silver engraved medallion the size of a large coin.

"It seems that she brought it with her from Edinburgh, her only possession of any value, found with her as a child on the street when she was taken in by the ladies at the 'Church.' It seemed to hold great meaning for her."

"A loan?"

"She is quite a determined young woman when she sets her mind to it," he added. "There was no dissuading her, and I will admit that I did extend more than the medallion is worth. However, I could not see her taking herself off with barely a farthing in her pocket."

I sat down in a nearby chair and stared at the letter.

"This is impossible," I finally found the words, aware that Brodie and Munro had arrived at Sussex Square as well. Brodie attempted to comfort me, his hand on my shoulder.

"She is not prepared..." I added, as if there was any point in arguing what was already done.

"She has to be found." I turned to Sir Laughton. "Did she say where she would be staying?"

He shook his head. "She said only that her friend worked at a tavern on the High Street in the Old Town."

Munro spoke for the first time since returning to Sussex Square.

"I will find her..."

Epilogue

BAKEHOUSE CLOSE, EDINBURGH, SCOTLAND

"DORA BROWN, YE SAY?" the old woman who had answered the door of the ground-floor flat inquired.

"That be the name she uses, but didna see her come in last night after her shift at the tavern, or the past few days, come to mind. Not unusual, if she had business elsewhere, if ye get my meanin'," she continued as she looked Lily up and down.

"A friend ye say? Yer not wot I usually see in this part of the Old Town."

Lily Montgomery nodded. "I've had a post from her."

"A post?" the woman hooted with laughter. "Didna know she knew how to write, but she is always good with her numbers. Them who ply the trade on their backsides learn their numbers quick.

"She mighta come in without me knowin' though, since the rents are due. She does that sometimes."

Lily inquired about Dora's flat number.

"Ye sure have a fine way of talkin'. I wouldna have guessed that Dora knew anyone so fancy. Hers is the first flat at the top of stairs. If she's there, ye tell her that I'm expectin' the rents."

"When pigs fly," Lily whispered to herself as she climbed the stairs.

The driver from Waverly Station had been reluctant to leave her at the address written in the note.

The tenement at the Close was like many she remembered from years before, along with the 'Church,' where both had worked. Although she had been merely a child when she was taken there to live and became a maid to the ladies who worked there.

Prostitution—the oldest profession in the world according to Lady Antonia Montgomery with whom she'd lived at Sussex Square in London the past several years.

It had surprised her that she knew so much about it. But perhaps it shouldn't have. Lady Montgomery had lived a very colourful life.

She was enormously fond of her and would be forever grateful to her. But most particularly, she owed everything to Mikaela Forsythe.

She admired her, considered her to be the family she had never known, along with Mr. Brodie. A chance encounter with Mikaela and Mr. Brodie, followed by the fire that had taken the 'Church,' and her life was changed.

Mikaela was intelligent, she had travelled widely, had learned a great many things from those travels, and lived her life on her own terms. Such as taking on the work of an inquiry agent with Mr. Brodie.

She would understand, Lily thought, as she found the door to that flat on the second floor.

She wasn't surprised by the poor conditions in that part of Edinburgh. All those years before she had lived with Dora and the other 'ladies' at the 'Church', a well-known brothel that was in Old Town as well.

Whatever the reason Dora had sent that brief note, she hoped that she might be able to help her now.

She knocked at the door. When there was no answer, she tried the latch. It was not bolted from the inside and the door slowly swung open. She called out, but there was no answer. She stepped inside the one room flat.

The building was old and there was no electricity. The only light came from the lamp at the end of the Close and spilled through the smudged panes of the window in the far wall. She called out once more.

Again, there was no answer. If Dora hadn't the rent money, she might indeed have spent the night some other place.

As she turned to leave, she caught a faint movement on the floor near the alcove where a curtain was drawn across. Then another movement, familiar from those years before when she had lived in such a place.

As she approached the alcove she saw it again, followed by the gleam of beady eyes. It was a rat. And not just one.

She pushed the curtain back and jumped back as several fled the body that lay on the floor beside the bed. She had found Dora.

Her hand covered her mouth as she stared down at her friend, her face swollen and bloodied.

She had seen bodies before, but this was her friend, and she kicked away a rat that attempted to return.

"Get on with ye!" she said, aware that it made no difference. Not now.

What had happened she thought as the tears came? Had Dora been attacked on the street and found her way back to the flat? Or had whoever was responsible followed her?

She thought of all the times Dora had protected her from

the other ladies but mostly from the men. She thought then of that note.

Who was her friend afraid of? What was it about? And now...?

"Hold on there!" the sharply barked order sliced through the horror and shock at what she had found.

"Turn around. Wot have we here?"

Lily slowly turned around and found herself face-to-face with a constable of the Edinburgh Police.

The telephone rang at the desk across from where Lily sat, presently a 'guest' of the Edinburgh Police after the information she had given them. Not that she was fooled by the temporary 'holding room' at the Central Police headquarters, the locked door, and the matron who had been left to watch over her.

She had been taken into custody after the encounter at Dora's flat. And had promptly informed the constable who wrote up the report at the central police station the name she had been given by Sir Laughton.

"If you should need assistance in any way," he had said when they last met. "It's always wise to know someone who might be helpful. Take this with you."

It was a note of introduction that explained her presence in Edinburgh.

That person's name was Alastair McQuarrie, a friend Sir Laughton had studied law with. The two had stayed in contact these many years since and had assisted one another in the past in legal matters.

She had been in Edinburgh less than a day, discovered her

friend, dead and was now being held as a *'person of interest'* in Dora's death. Not precisely what she had hoped for.

The telephone continued to ring, and a matron reappeared from an adjacent room—a prune-faced woman Lily was convinced if she had smiled her face would crack and fall to pieces on the floor. A definite improvement to her way of thinking.

The woman answered the phone. The conversation was brief, with a quick look in Lily's direction.

"I understand," she replied and returned the handset to the cradle.

"You are to be released," she was informed. The woman sounded almost disappointed.

Lily stood, grateful for what had to be Mr. MacQuarrie's intervention, and gathered her travel bag as the door to the holding room opened.

She told herself that she must remember to send a note of gratitude both to Mr. MacQuarrie and Sir Laughton in London once she returned.

She looked up. The smile on her face immediately disappeared as she stared at a familiar face.

"What the devil are ye doin' here?" she demanded.

"I was sent to rescue an insolent piece of baggage, and bring ye back to London," Munro snapped back at her as he handed the matron the necessary paperwork for her release.

Lily fought to compose herself.

"I do not need to be rescued!" she informed him, which no doubt seemed somewhat questionable at the moment. Not that she would admit it. "And I am not returning to London!"

· · ·

Munro took her by the arm and dragged her from the holding room at the Central Police Station, a place he was more than familiar with and had no intention of remaining longer.

James Alec Munro cursed. He'd taken on the task of finding the girl and escorting her back to London.

He'd succeeded in finding her with information provided by Sir Laughton, who was Lady Montgomery's attorney. He had not expected that he would find her in police custody. Mr. McQuarrie had assisted with getting her released.

Lily pulled free from his grasp as they reached the street.

"I said no!"

Icy rain had set in, and the chit of a girl stood there like a fire-breathin' dragon. Munro cursed as he waved down a coach.

"Ye will go!"

She stubbornly refused.

"My friend is dead! I intend to find who killed her. You would do the same!"

I hope you enjoyed DEADLY REVENGE.

The modern era of law establishment began with the creation of the Metropolitan Police by Sir Robert Peel in 1829. Hence the nickname "bobbies" after Sir Robert, or Peelers. And not always in the most polite terms.

It was originally a force that consisted of 1,000 constables, tasked with preventing crime merely by their presence about London in uniforms.

Inspectors were allowed to carry weapons—firearms— while constables such as Joseph Martin in DEADLY REVENGE usually carried a short stick called a truncheon. Constables were organized into divisions around London, and then expanded with a separate police force to cover the financial district, which was plagued by a high incidence of crime.

It was this organization that Brodie stepped into in 1874, working the streets with his experience in street crime from the other side of the law, and eventually working his way up to inspector. During this time, he walked the patrol with Constable Martin and formed a deep respect.

There are few he trusts, and Constable Martin was one. He feels the loss deeply, one more among many as the series has expanded. There will be more challenges ahead.

Mikaela has experienced losses as well, and now the townhouse at Mayfair, her sanctuary as I described it. Bricks and stones that can be replaced, but it represents a change for her. One of her new challenges will be living at the office on the Strand, not an ideal situation, but she is up to the challenge.

One challenge she is not pleased with is a joint investigation that may develop with a man by the name of Holmes at the insistence of the Home Secretary in a particularly complicated case.

The crime sheet that I have referred to was a part of the Times newspaper, a daily update on crime throughout London, usually written in somewhat cryptic details, as one might expect.

I've chosen to embellish that somewhat by describing it as sensationalism with the purpose of promoting readership, while, at the same time, assuring the public that crime is under control.

This could prove quite interesting, as the man behind those articles posted on the crime sheet, Theodolphus Burke, might well find himself the subject of one of those lurid, sensational articles.

The public works boot that I've used as a clue was part of the attire worn by prisoners. It had a V-cut in the heel.

The First Earl of Oxford, Sir Asquith, was appointed Home Secretary in 1892. His responsibilities will increasingly include home-grown terrorism, which will draw Brodie and Munro into his efforts to find the perpetrators among a group of men who belong to a secret organization.

And how might that include Lady Antonia Montgomery,

who has shown a fascination with Brodie and Mikaela's inquiry cases, and is fearless at her advanced age?

She is not one to meddle, however she is convinced that she has certain experience that can be important to them.

And then there is Mikaela's ward, Lily. A child no longer, extremely intelligent, clever, and highly educated with experience from their cases.

And coming soon...my new series with Book 1 following Lily's adventures as she is drawn back to Edinburgh, and the life she was forced into there as a maid to the ladies at a brothel called the 'Church.'

It is a search for her own past that begins with a letter she receives, then quickly becomes dangerous when the friend who sent that letter and was one of the 'ladies' is murdered.

Munro takes on the responsibility of bringing her back to London, but quickly discovers that it is easier said than done.

The 'child' who first arrived from Edinburgh is now a strong-willed young woman, with secrets of her own. Secrets that will be difficult for him to understand or accept as he is forced to work with her to learn the reason her friend was murdered, and she fights that inner voice that both terrifies and fascinates her, and what that voice means about her past.

MURDER BY DEATH, BOOK 1, Lily Montgomery and James Munro Murder Mystery (yes, he has a first name!)

They are reluctant partners who must trust one another if they are to survive as they are drawn into the secrets of the past.

"Are ye a witch then?" Munro demands as they discover a bloodied body. "Do ye conjure things out of the air, like the Kelpies?"

"If I was, I would turn you into the horse's ass that you are!" Lily replies as she searches the body.

A man who needs no one and a young woman in search of

her past, forced to rely upon one another to unravel those secrets, and...

Also by Carla Simpson

Angus Brodie and Mikaela Forsythe Murder Mystery

A Deadly Affair

Deadly Secrets

A Deadly Game

Deadly Illusion

A Deadly Vow

Deadly Obsession

A Deadly Deception

A Deadly Betrayal

A Deadly Scandal

Deadly Lies

Deadly Curse

Deadly Ghost

Deadly Attraction

Deadly Murder

Deadly Revenge

Merlin Series

Daughter of Fire

Daughter of the Mist

Daughter of the Light

Shadows of Camelot

Dawn of Camelot

Daughter of Camelot

The Young Dragons, Blood Moon

Clan Fraser

Betrayed

Revenge

Outlaws, Scoundrels & Lawmen

Desperado's Caress

Passion's Splendor

Silver Mistress

Memory and Desire

Desire's Flame

Silken Surrender

Angels, Devils, Rebels & Rogues

Ravished

Always My Love

Seductive Caress

Seduced

Deceived

About the Author

"I want to write a book ..." she said.

"Then do it," he said.

And she did, and received two offers for that first book proposal.

A dozen historical romances later, and a prophecy from a gifted psychic and the Legacy Series was created, expanding to seven additional titles.

Along the way, two film options, and numerous book awards.

But wait, there's more a voice whispered, after a trip to Scotland and a visit to the standing stones in the far north, and as old as Stonehenge, sign posts the voice told her, and the Clan Fraser books that have followed that told the beginnings of the clan and the family she was part of ...

And now ... murder and mystery set against the backdrop of Victorian London in the new Angus Brodie and Mikaela Forsythe series, with an assortment of conspirators and murderers in the brave new world after the Industrial Revolution where terrorists threaten and the world spins closer to war.

When she is not exploring the Darkness of the fantasy world, or pursuing ancestors in ancient Scotland, she lives in the mountains near Yosemite National Park with bears and mountain lions, and plots murder and revenge.

And did I mention fierce, beautiful women and dangerous, handsome men?

They're there, waiting ...

Join Carla's Newsletter

9 798900 430485